LONDON'S BURNING

LONDON'S BURNING

BEHIND THE SCENES WITH BRITAIN'S FAVOURITE FIREFIGHTERS

GEOFF TIBBALLS

BOXTREE

LWT

ACKNOWLEDGEMENTS

This book would not have been possible without the assistance of Paul Knight and the cast and crew of *London's Burning*. So the author would like to thank the following for their friendly co-operation and guidance: Producers Paul Knight and Jack Rosenthal, Directors Gerry Mill, John Reardon and Keith Washington, Production Designer Colin Monk, Stunt Co-ordinator Alf Joint, Directors of Photography Geoff Harrison and Paul Bond, Fire Brigade Liaison Officer Nobby Clark, Casting Director Corinne Rodriguez, Production Supervisor Chris Hall, Supervising Editor Frank Webb, Special Effects Supervisors Tom Harris and David Harris, Senior Writer and Story Consultant Anita Bronson, Writers David Humphries and Roger Marshall, Wardrobe Supervisor Lynnette Cummin, Location Managers Kevin Holden and Malcolm Treen, Construction Manager John Carman, Property Buyer Will Hinton, Property Master Ray Holt, Stills Photographers Mike Vaughan, Graham Attwood, Simon Farrell and Tony Russell, LWT Publicity Officer Vanda Rumney and Picture Editor Shane Chapman, the Press Office of the London Fire Brigade and all the cast, past and present. Thanks also to Boxtree Senior Editor Rod Green and, last but by no means least, to Paul Knight's assistant Patsy Lightfoot for all her hard work in fixing up the interviews.

First published in the UK in 1992
by Boxtree Ltd., Broadwall House, 21 Broadwall,
London SE1 9PL

10 9 8 7 6 5 4 3 2 1

Designed and typeset by Blackjacks, London
Cover Design by Paterson Jones
Additional artwork by Dave Bull
Picture research by Shane Chapman and Geoff Tibballs

Printed and bound in Italy by OFSA s.p.a.

A catalogue record for this book is available from the British Library

ISBN - 1 85283 731 4

INTRODUCTION
By Paul Knight, Producer of London's Burning

In 1986 I was approached by Linda Agran, who was then the Deputy Controller of Drama at London Weekend Television, to produce a new film by Jack Rosenthal. It was based on Jack's long-standing friendship with a fireman and was triggered by the rioting at Broadwater Farm where PC Blakelock was tragically murdered and where, for the first time, the Fire Brigade came under attack. The script was called *London's Burning* and I immediately thought it was a wonderful piece of writing.

Six years on and *London's Burning* has gone from strength to strength. It has set the ratings alight. Jack's original film drew an audience of 12.5 million, and last year's dramatic finale to the fourth series was enjoyed by no fewer than 18.9 million viewers.

Why has *London's Burning* been so successful? For a start it came along at a time when there was great sensitivity in the television industry towards violence. There was a backlash against shows like *Dempsey and Makepeace* and *Miami Vice* So a series about the Fire Brigade was ideal – plenty of action but no violence. After all, firefighters do a lot of good – they don't go around shooting people. Having said that, nobody really knew exactly what the Fire Brigade did. This was new territory for television. We all knew about the police from shows like *The Bill* and about the ambulance service from programmes such as *Casualty* but there had never been a television series about the Fire Brigade. The idea had been mooted many times over the years but the reason Jack Rosenthal's film worked was that he instilled plenty of humour. This gave it that vital edge.

Reality is the keynote of *London's Burning* and we couldn't have achieved it without the tremendous help of the London Fire Brigade. The first thing we did when making the original film was to go and see the then Deputy Chief Officer of the London Fire Brigade Gerry Clarkson (he later became Chief Officer). He took what I think was a massive gamble on us. He was an admirer of Jack Rosenthal's work but it was still amazing that he offered us such co-operation including the use of a fully operational fire station. That original meeting with the Brigade to ask permission for the film was the most diffi-cult I've ever had in my life. Gerry didn't pull any punches and emphasised that he expected us to stick by our mandate which was to make a good film which would show the operational side of the Fire Brigade absolutely correctly. He understood that as it was drama – warts and all – it wouldn't be a glorifi-cation of the London Fire Brigade.

To ensure that the operational side was totally authentic, he appointed Brian 'Nobby' Clark as our Fire Brigade Liaison Officer. Nobby is with us at all times. He becomes very involved in the technical side because none of us, although we've been working on the series for several years, really understands precisely what the Fire Brigade's reaction would be in certain circumstances – even simply what firefighters

would do in a given situation. Detail is all important; our actors even attend Fire Brigade training school before each series so that they look the part on screen.

Like many of the original team, Nobby has been with us ever since. *London's Burning* is very much a team effort. For instance we have kept the same directors, designer and direc-tors of photography. These people understand the show and have a very good relationship with the Fire Brigade. What's more, they know how to shoot fire.

An important decision I made when LWT gave the go ahead for a series was that it should have a serial element. Viewers would tune in to find out what happened to the characters from week to week. It was important to show their private lives – you can't do an hour a week just fighting fires. But we try to avoid getting over-soapy and attempt to keep *London's Burning* full of incident at work and at home.

London's Burning reflects the humour and perils of being a firefighter. It's a dangerous job and *London's Burning* is a very dangerous series to make. We've shown countless fires, we've rescued people from high-rise buildings, cranes and sewers. We've had a trench collapse, a coach crash, we even turned over a fire appliance. Every episode has a major incident. We use real off-duty firefighters in the most hazardous fire scenes and we always have a standby fire crew in attendance as safety cover. We have a very good stunt team – obviously we don't want to lose too many actors. But despite all the precautions, we've had a few lucky escapes over the years.

Our relationship with the London Fire Brigade remains very close. The new Chief Officer Brian Robinson supports the series in the same way as his predecessor Gerry Clarkson. They realise it is good PR for the Brigade because it has heightened the public's awareness of what they do. And what they do is save lives. For as *London's Burning* shows, today's firefighters are genuine heroes.

1 STARTING THE FIRE

Strange as it may seem, *London's Burning* owes its existence to a Swiss au pair girl. Her name was Ruth and back in 1978 she was in the employ of multi-award winning writer Jack Rosenthal and his actress wife Maureen Lipman, helping to look after their young children Amy and Adam. Ruth's boyfriend was a London fireman, Les Murphy.

'When Ruth and Les got married,' recalls Jack Rosenthal, 'they lived with us for a year. Very often Les would come back from a night watch just as I was coming down in the morning and we'd sit at the table with a coffee and talk. He'd tell me things that had happened that night. Sometimes he'd be depressed and occasionally elated.'

Until he met Les Murphy, Rosenthal admits that, like most of the public who had never needed to summon the Brigade with a frantic 999 call, his view of firemen was faintly comic. 'My attitude to firemen seemed to have been coloured by a sort of cartoon mythology which pigeon holed them with ancient Enid Blyton postmen on bikes and long-gone village coppers on their beat. You saw a fire-engine clanging down the High Street – and your immediate reaction was to smile.

'I'm not sure why this was. Maybe it was because – just as civil servants are traditionally supposed to drink tea all day – firemen are supposed to slide down poles. Maybe it was because they rescued cats from trees. Or maybe there was an even simpler reason: that they really did grow up to become what we only said we would.'

As Les Murphy continued to drop round once a week, Rosenthal learned more and more about the real life of a fireman. 'Les would pop round to do all sorts of errands and odd jobs for me – like fixing the car, mowing the lawn or shifting the odd wardrobe. He told me stories of the tragedies, the wheezes, the mess-table dramas of his daily life.'

These stories, together with horrifyingly graphic television news pictures about terrorist atrocities and such disasters as the 1985 Bradford City football ground fire in which 52 people died, brought home the harsh reality of a fireman's life. The cartoon mythology had gone up in flames.

'With each story, I realised more and more that the Fire Brigade was not only a whole world of its own,' says Rosenthal, 'but a uniquely dramatic one of clashing opposites. Firefighters are unique in that, unlike soldiers or policemen to whom danger and possible death are a virtual raison d'etre, they are civilians. They don't face flick-knives, guns or bombs. They live at home with their families and go off to work like the rest of us.

'And there the similarity stops dead. Across the threshold is no man's land. Beyond that could be the nightmare of the fire at King's Cross. At any moment in the next eight hours they might be fighting for people's lives in a literal hell of pitch-black smoke and searing infernos. Mostly they win, sometimes they lose. Then they go home like the rest of us, cursing the traffic jams and wondering what's on telly tonight. Their day's

The Fire Brigade tackle another incident, or shout, as they call them.

work is behind them and forgotten – or, more truthfully, half-forgotten. There's one exception. The memory of a child's corpse never goes away.'

It was listening to Murphy's tales or, just as often, wanting to hear the ones he was too exhausted, modest or upset to tell, that made Jack Rosenthal want to write something about the Fire Brigade. But what? He had enough material for ten documentaries, enough tragedy for a series of mini-series and enough fun for a long-running comedy. He decided to concentrate all three elements into one TV film.

Then one night of tragic violence in October 1985 spurred Rosenthal into action and gave him the framework for his film. That was when PC Keith Blakelock was brutally hacked to death during riots on the Broadwater Farm Estate in Tottenham – riots which for the first time saw London's firefighters come under attack.

'For a long time before the riot itself, Broadwater Farm had become a minefield for firemen. Often the Brigade would be lured inside by hoax 999 calls. Once there, they'd be bombarded with paving-stones dropped from the balconies. To the small core of hard men of the ghetto, a fireman's uniform represented the same badge of authority as a policeman's – and provoked the same hatred. PC Blakelock was in the act of protecting firemen when he was ambushed.'

The second key factor in moulding Rosenthal's screenplay was his decision to introduce a woman. At the time there were only about half a dozen women firefighters in the London Fire Brigade. 'I'd read press reports about the men's animosity towards having a woman on the watch,' says Rosenthal, 'how they claimed that their wives wouldn't like the idea of them working with women, how some thought that including women would deprive the job of its heroic image, and it seemed an interesting line to explore.'

To beef up his knowledge of the London Fire Brigade, Rosenthal gained first-hand experience by going on shouts with the men from Hornsey Fire Station. 'I lived with them for two days and a night and I also rode with the men from the Fire Brigade's elite team at Shaftesbury Avenue which covers the "fire-a-minute" square mile of Soho. Both stations were very receptive. Their only concern was that I was insured because naturally enough they didn't want to have to foot the bill if I was hurt.'

Rosenthal also saw the other side to a firefighter's day. For it's not all alarm bells. Between shouts there is equipment to be maintained, the station to be kept clean, drill to be done. And there are wheezes. 'These painstakingly elaborate, often ingenious, often cruel practical jokes are probably what keep firefighters sane,' says Rosenthal, 'or mad enough to do the job they do.

'This double life of extremes – tragedy and farce, heroism and silliness – breeds more opposites: a compassion for the victims of fires and no sympathy whatever for each other. A firefighter, wolfing his statutory cheese and onion rolls at the Mess table, wouldn't dream of saying he had a headache or he couldn't pay his mortgage or his wife was leaving him. At best, he'd get half a dozen Coke cans hurled straight at his headache, he'd be told to go and live in a tent, and his mates would ask for his wife's new phone number. If he was fool enough to show that any of these upset him even more, they'd keep it up for anything between six months and a lifetime.'

As befits a writer of his stature, Rosenthal's homework for his new project went far beyond spending a few days at fire stations. He listened to officers from Brigade Headquarters, met black firefighters, women firefighters, Rastafarians and residents of Broadwater Farm. And he closely observed the reactions of the public at each incident.

Having decided that the centrepiece of the film would be a riot, Rosenthal set about drawing up his characters. 'I wouldn't say any of the characters were based on any particular individual – instead they were an amalgamation of the various firefighters I'd met. I was particularly attracted to the way most members of the watch are given nicknames. I love nicknames and it took me back to the days when I wrote a comedy series called *The Dustbinmen* with characters like Heavy Breathing and Cheese and Egg.'

Thus were born Bayleaf (because he was the mess manager), Charisma (because he hadn't got any), Vaseline (because he was slippery), Sicknote (because he was a hypochondriac), Rambo (because he was the Watch's action man) and Ethnic, the one black firefighter on Blue Watch.

Ethnic was the key character in Rosenthal's script as the riot erupted on the very estate where Ethnic lived with his parents. The writer explains: 'At the same time Ethnic felt loyalty both to his ghetto community and to his fellow firefighters. The point I was trying to make was that the whole subject of civil disorder is very complicated and there are no easy solutions. What the film tried to do was show that there can be faults on both sides. The fault lies in society and the fact that there are ghettos. What is patently wrong, though, is that firemen should be the subject of attack.'

Jack Rosenthal's screenplay was commissioned by Euston Films' Linda Agran and when Agran moved to London Weekend Television to become deputy controller of drama, she took it with her. LWT's programme controller at the time was John Birt who liked the script so much that he quickly gave the go-ahead for it to be made into a film. Agran then approached producer Paul Knight, fresh from finishing the third series of

The boys (and girl) from Blue Watch.

Robin of Sherwood where he had gained a certain experience of fire by burning down sundry Saxon villages. Over a period of nigh on 20 years, Paul Knight had established a reputation as one of the most accomplished producers of popular drama with credits including *The Adventures of Black Beauty, The Crezz, Dick Turpin* and *Robin of Sherwood* (he has since added *Pulaski* and *The Accountant* which won the 1990 BAFTA award for Best Single Drama).

Paul Knight enjoyed the script enormously. 'I think what impressed me most,' he says, 'was that it wasn't just a documentary/drama about the Fire Brigade. The madness and humour lightened it.'

One of Paul Knight's first calls was to director Les Blair. 'I had been impressed by his film-making over a number of years especially the controversial G.F. Newman series *Law and Order* which had upset police and prison officers in 1978. I had always wanted to work with Les and he too enjoyed the script so I employed him as director.'

The most urgent requirement was to obtain the co-operation of the London Fire Brigade. After that meeting, Deputy Chief Officer Gerry Clarkson appointed Nobby Clark, who was then the uniformed Station Officer in the press office of the London Fire Brigade, to be the Brigade's advisor on the film. Nobby Clark says: 'When Mr Clarkson agreed that the Brigade would assist strictly on the understanding that the film would be warts and all, I remember thinking, as a press officer, "That sounds risky."'

Jack Rosenthal realised he had found his true vocation when he wrote his life story at the tender age of nine. True, it was only one line and was done on a rubber-stamp printing set but it's the thought that counts.

Born in Manchester in 1931, Rosenthal's first proper literary offering was a sketch for wartime radio comedienne Suzette Tarri. 'It was duly returned by the BBC,' he reflects wistfully.

After reading English and Russian at Sheffield University, he did two years' National Service in the Royal Navy before joining the research department at Granada Television in the early days of ITV.

In 1962 he was part of the writing team for the pioneering Saturday night satire *That Was The Week That Was*, the show that became the scourge of the political and the pompous. He also contributed to series as diverse as the Arthur Lowe comedy *Pardon the Expression* and the cult police drama *The Odd Man*.

But it was in the field of comedy that Jack Rosenthal really made his name. The adventures of a motley bunch of refuse collectors, *The Dustbinmen*, and their dustcart Thunderbird Three, shot to the top of the ratings in 1969. The following year saw the debut of *The*

Lovers, the memorable tale of young romantics Geoffrey and Beryl. *The Lovers* earned Jack the Writers' Guild Best Comedy Series Award and led to a film spin-off.

Since then, the awards haven't stopped flowing. His hilarious play about Sunday morning football, *Another Sunday & Sweet F.A.*, won the TV Critics' Best Play Award for 1972. Among his other successes have been *The Evacuees* (British Academy Best Play Award, Broadcasting Press Guild Best Play Award, International Emmy Award, 1975); *Bar Mitzvah Boy* (British Academy Best Play Award, Broadcasting Press Guild Best Play Award, 1976);

Ready When You Are, Mr McGill (British Academy Best Play Nomination 1976); *Spend, Spend, Spend*, the story of pools winner Viv Nicholson (British Academy Best Play Award and Italia Prize Nomination, 1977), *The Knowledge*, which starred Mick Ford as a would-be London taxi driver (British Academy Best Play Nomination and Italia Prize Nomination, 1979); and *P'Tang, Yang, Kipperbang* (British Academy Best Play Nomination, 1982). He recently wrote a couple of episodes for *About Face* which starred his actress wife Maureen Lipman.

His feature films include *The Chain*, *Lucky Star* and *Yentl*, the latter co-written with Barbra Streisand.

For all his triumphs, Jack Rosenthal does have a confession to make. He has blood on his hands. It dates back to 1961 when he became one of a quartet of regular writers for Granada's promising new serial *Coronation Street*. In all he wrote around 150 episodes and in 1967 actually produced the Street for six months. It was during that time that he was forced to commit a heinous crime. 'I had Elsie Tanner marry US army sergeant Steve Tanner and then in the same episode I killed off Harry Hewit. In some quarters I don't think I've ever been forgiven for killing off poor old Harry!'

The Brigade's co-operation extended to providing two fully-equipped fire appliances seconded from its spare fleet and a real fire station. But finding the right station was no easy matter. Nobby Clark recalls: 'I spent quite a while going through all the Brigade properties that were no longer used. I came up with a shopping list of old places and took out Paul Knight, Les Blair and the designer Colin Monk. We trailed all over London. Some of the stations had been vandalised or had squatters and were in a bit of a state. One by one they were rejected and we ended up at the old East Greenwich fire station which was right by an elevated section of main road. I picked up the vibes that this was not what they wanted so I said, "Give me an idea of what you do want."

'They said, "We want a fire station that's not on a main road so it's quiet, we want a large yard for the film crew and it needs to have character." Although about 90 per cent of fire stations are on main roads, I thought I knew the ideal place for them – Dockhead on the south of the river in the shadow of the Tower of London. As we turned the corner, Colin Monk saw the front and I think the decision was made that this was the right one before we even got into the yard. The problem was, it was an operational fire station, very much in everyday use...'

While that difficulty was being overcome, the matter of casting Blue Watch had to be sorted out, a task performed by Paul Knight, Les Blair and LWT's casting director at the time, Corinne Rodriguez. Paul Knight was very clear about the type of actors he wanted.

Katherine Rogers blazed a trail as Josie.

'We wanted people who hadn't been seen a lot on television. The essence of the film was that it had to have a documentary feel, one of absolute reality and you can't get that using people who are familiar from *Coronation Street* or whatever. The only person who had previously enjoyed much TV exposure was James Hazeldine but he hadn't done any long-running series and we needed him as the senior hand to be weightier than the others. Bayleaf is the one who's been in the Brigade a number of years, who's seen it all, done it all. Jimmy fitted the bill very well. But the rest were all unknowns.'

Over a period of a month, the casting team saw more than 100 actors. Many of them read around a table in groups, forming a kind of Watch, to see how they reacted with one another. Eventually they were whittled down to the original Watch – James Marcus as Tate, Sean Blowers as Hallam, James Hazeldine as Bayleaf, Mark Arden as Vaseline, Rupert Baker as Malcolm, Jerome Flynn as Rambo, Gerard Horan as Charisma, Gary McDonald as Ethnic, Katharine Rogers as Josie and Richard Walsh as Sicknote.

Corinne Rodriguez, now head of casting for the Royal Shakespeare Company but still the casting director on *London's Burning*, says the most difficult character to cast was undoubtedly Josie. 'She had to have so many varying attributes. She had to be tough and working-class, she had to be over 5ft. 6in. tall (the Fire Brigade's minimum height) and before filming she had to go on a rigorous training course. There aren't too many actresses who regularly work out in gyms so we were really lucky to find Kath Rogers.'

As part of his preparation, director Les Blair visited a number of fire stations in an effort to familiarise himself with the rituals of the Watch. He happened to be at a station when there was a huge fire at the News International plant in London's Dockland. 'I thought this is going to be really good – a really big fire but although there were 30 engines and it was as spectacular as the fire in *Gone With The Wind*, all the firemen could do was pump water on it. I discovered that they hate fires like that. To them, firefighting means going into houses, not putting water on to

Jerome Flynn played the appropriately-named Rambo in the original London's Burning *film.*

something. Yet when I said, "Don't you get fed up rescuing cats on roofs?" they said, "We don't mind. A cat means something to an old lady."'

Before filming could start, the problem of making a major television programme at a working fire station had to be addressed. It wasn't as if the 80-strong crew would only be there for a few days – filming spanned six weeks. What would happen when the emergency bells went down half-way through a 'take'? The Brigade answer calls immedi-

Food for thought.

The spectacular motorway crash in fog in series five was staged on an unopened section of the A3(M) near Liss in Hampshire. For the pile-up, Property Buyer Will Hinton bought no fewer than 39 vehicles – 'four articulated trucks, two lorries, six vans and the rest were assorted mashed vehicles. I also had to find a place that does tarmac and somewhere that sells central reservation barriers that aren't new. It was an interesting shopping list!'

The fog effect was created by a series of fog machines, placed in a circle so that no matter which way the wind blew, there would still be some fog hanging around. And because the nearest water supply was two-thirds of a mile away in a village, a hoseline had to be run all the way from the village to the scene of the crash. Otherwise Blue Watch wouldn't have been able to put out the blazes.

ately so there was no question of the director asking them to wait until he had finished that scene, thereby risking burning down half of London. Nor was it exactly desirable for the appliances to ride roughshod over everything and everyone barring their exit, in the process probably damaging thousands of pounds of equipment not to mention a few members of Equity.

So LWT provided a highly sophisticated, radio-equipped Portakabin in the yard at Dockhead. The real firefighters prevented South-East London from going up in flames from there while the TV Brigade took over the station itself, re-christening it Blackwall although Dockhead is in fact some four miles west of Blackwall Tunnel. Incidentally, Jack Rosenthal's screenplay was based on Southgate Fire Station which meant that the script had to be altered slightly to accommodate the different layout of Dockhead.

The men from Dockhead were incredibly helpful. They willingly gave up their mess hall (true, in exchange for free meals with cast and crew in the LWT catering truck) and even came and went about their emergencies as quietly as possible during filming. They silenced the station bells, manoeuvred their vehicles out by the back gates and didn't switch on their two-tone horns until they were as far down the road as safety permitted.

Filming began in July 1986 and five months later, on 7 December, the two-hour film of *London's Burning* was transmitted. Jack Rosenthal's renowned humour (spendidly illustrated in Vaseline's wedding scene to his third wife, cruelly interrupted by the arrival of his irate second spouse, warning about the perils of marrying a fireman, particularly that fireman) cleverly combined with tragedy (the brutal murder of Ethnic at the height of the riot), captivated the nation. With a budget of over £1 million, it was at the time the most expensive film ever made by LWT but it proved to be money well spent.

The critics loved it. *The Independent* summed up: 'This wildly funny, adventurous and moving play was one of the big events of the year's TV.' In the *Daily Telegraph*, Charles Clover wrote: 'Rosenthal has one of the canniest ears for dialogue around, and he was excelling himself.' The *Mail On Sunday* described it as 'rich, satisfying, authentic and moving' while *Today* called it 'an outstanding piece of contemporary drama.' Twelve and a half million viewers agreed. It was nominated for a prestigious BAFTA award in the Best Single Film category. 'We didn't get it,' reflects Paul Knight, 'but it was nice to be nominated.' *London's Burning* was indeed hot stuff.

Not surprisingly in view of the affection bestowed on their baby, LWT gave the go-ahead for a series of *London's Burning*. Paul Knight was duly approached by Linda Agran to produce the series and has masterminded the show ever since with Nick Elliott,

Actress Samantha Beckinsale (who plays Kate Stevens) receives her diploma for completing the real Fire Brigade training course.

LWT's current head of drama, succeeding Linda Agran as executive producer. But back in 1987 Paul Knight was confronted with two major obstacles – finding a location and finding some writers.

'It was obvious that we couldn't shoot an entire series at a working station like Dockhead,' says Knight, 'so I asked production designer Colin Monk to build an exact replica of the interior of Dockhead, apart from the appliance bay which occupied the ground floor. The set was built at the LWT studios in Penarth Street which had been used for *Dempsey and Makepeace* and where the first series of *London's Burning* was to be made.'

The other problem was that Jack Rosenthal was not interested in writing for the series. 'So I had to approach new writers which meant reading a lot of possible scripts. In the end, I decided to use two writers – Tony Hoare (who'd done a lot of work on *Minder*) and a little later Anita Bronson who was then quite inexperienced as a series writer. There was an initial suggestion that the series should consist of a one-off film every week which tied up comfortably but I was against that. I decided that the series should have a serial element and I think that was the most fundamentally important decision that we made. What happened to the characters could therefore be developed over a series. The characters needed to be able to expand.'

Of necessity, there were also cast changes at the start of the first series. Paul Knight continues: 'We wanted to bring in another black fireman to replace Ethnic so we created Tony, played by Treva Etienne. Meanwhile Jerome Flynn, who played Rambo in the film, was not available. At the auditions for Rambo, it had been a close thing between Jerome Flynn and an actor named Glen Murphy. It was a very difficult choice but Jerome shaded it because he'd had a little more acting experience. But Corinne Rodriguez and I remembered Glen and I got the writers to create the role of George, an ex-boxer and in many ways a similar character to Rambo. So Glen finally made it on to *London's Burning* as George. And still in that first episode, Ross Boatman was introduced as Kevin Medhurst.'

Since then, there have been quite a few changes among the members of Blue Watch. Vaseline, Charisma, Tony, Josie and Tate have departed and been replaced by Kate, Colin, Nick and Recall. 'We need changes of personnel,' says Paul Knight, 'because in reality the Fire Brigade do change personnel a lot. Usually we do it because an actor wants to leave to go off to do other things but there was one occasion that was different.

'I decided that in the second series we needed to lose a fireman. I thought it was important that we showed that because of the amount of danger these men were being involved in on a weekly basis, things can go wrong. It would be wrong if everybody came out of it unscathed every week. It seemed to me that, sadly, we had to show somebody dying.

'Having looked at the Watch very carefully, I came to the conclusion that the person we should kill off should be Vaseline – not because I didn't think Mark Arden was a wonderful actor (in fact he's probably one of the best comedy actors in the country) but because I needed somebody who was going to have a terrific effect on the audience. What helped matters slightly was that Mark also had other work in the pipeline and was starting to build his own career. Even so it was a very difficult thing to tell him he was being killed off. It's not a nice thing to tell someone.

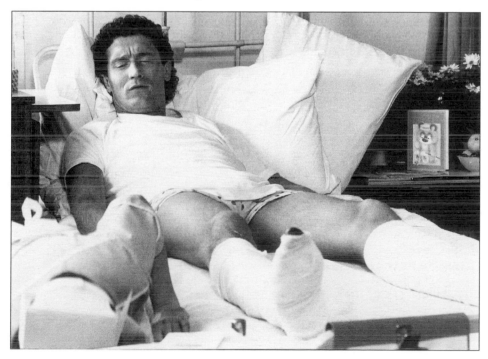

Vaseline was seriously injured when his boots caught fire in the first series, but was to suffer a worse fate in the second...

Another day, another victim to be rescued by Kate Stevens and Blue Watch.

'So we killed Vaseline in an accident at the docks. What it has meant is that nobody at home is quite sure now, when we do fires and dangerous incidents, whether everyone will come out alive. And that is vital if the series is to have any credibility.'

Of the others who have quit *London's Burning*, the luckiest was Gerard Horan who played Charisma. Paul Knight says: 'Gerard was offered the opportunity to go on a world tour with Kenneth Branagh's company, which he'd always wanted to do, so he left. I would possibly have killed Charisma instead of Vaseline but I didn't know Gerard was leaving until after the event.'

The departure of Katharine Rogers as Josie came as something of a surprise but Corinne Rodriguez found an ideal replacement in Samantha Beckinsale as Kate Stevens. 'I'd worked with Sam's father Richard in the play *Funny Peculiar*,' recalls Corinne, 'and he was just about to do an Agatha Christie film for LWT when he died. Because I'd known Richard, I kept an eye on Sam's career and watched her in a fringe play. When it came to looking for a successor to Kath Rogers, I thought of her. She was very different to Kath, which was important, and what's more she worked out in gyms so I thought she'd be able to handle the physical demands of the show.'

Six years and 42 programmes after Jack Rosenthal's trailblazing film, *London's Burning* is more popular than ever. Viewing figures have risen steadily over the first four series. The first averaged 12.1 million, the second 12.3 million, the third 12.5 million and the fourth 15 million. Its success is a tribute to the way in which television and Fire Brigade have worked together. Paul Knight is justifiably proud of having balanced outstanding drama with total authenticity. 'We're not here to glamorise the Brigade,' he says, 'but we do try to get it right technically. I hope they trust us.'

2 FROM SCRIPT TO SCREEN

The headquarters of *London's Burning* is Jacob Street Studios, about half a mile from Tower Bridge. It used to be a flour factory with a demolition order hanging over it and is approached by streets barely wide enough to take a small family saloon let alone a cumbersome fire appliance. (Author's note: they don't call them fire engines any more.) With its cramped offices and sundry Portakabins, Paramount Studios it isn't.

London's Burning moved to Jacob Street from LWT's Penarth Street studios for the start of the second series. Penarth Street was to be re-developed and Paul Knight spent two or three months looking for an alternative studio. He examined a number of likely warehouses before deciding that Jacob Street had everything he wanted. And, most important of all, it was no more than a decent length of hose from Dockhead Fire Station, the model for Blackwall.

Designer Colin Monk's immaculate replica of the upper floor of Dockhead is now a permanent set at Jacob Street. It includes the mess kitchen, rest room, a fully-tiled shower room, offices and dormitories, complete with uncomfortable-looking beds. Peer through the windows and all you find is a painted backcloth of blocks of flats. What would Lloyd Grossman make of a place like this? The mess kitchen is of particular interest. There are big ovens, heavy-duty pans, a microwave, a sink, cutlery, crockery, a couple of toasters and even a large sack of onions, presumably in reserve for emotional scenes. And near the entrance to the studio there is a 7ft pole for the TV firefighters to slide down en route to a shout. Incidentally, the pole at Dockhead is 18ft high. There is one other major difference between the Jacob Street set and Dockhead – the walls on the set are removable. For about six months a year, *London's Burning* uses five of the six studios at Jacob Street (among the other visitors are *Spitting Image*).

One for the album – the London's Burning *cast and crew at Jacob Street.*

Being next door to Dockhead is not only convenient, it saves a bit on the budget which currently stands at over £500,000 per episode. Paul Knight says: 'We film quite often at Dockhead and use their appliance bay and yard a lot. But Dockhead is still a working fire station and before any scene is set up, they move the appliances outside ready to answer any emergency calls.'

Although filming a series of *London's Burning* takes only six months, it is in essence an all-year round operation. In fact there is a period of 18 months between the initial discussions and a series actually hitting the screen. 'What happens,' says Paul Knight, 'is that towards the end of the series we're filming, I sit down first with Anita Bronson, who is now our senior writer and story consultant, and then with Nobby Clark, our Fire Brigade advisor, and we talk about what we'd like to see happen in the next series. We have a head-banging session which can go on for two or three days about the ideas we have for the characters. Nobby gets all the cuttings from the Brigade Press Office so we have a stack of cuttings of real incidents which he files and sorts out.'

Nobby Clark works on the storylines in the 'close season'. 'I go through the press cuttings and also draw on my own knowledge, taking pieces from one or two stories and linking them together. Virtually every incident in *London's Burning* has really happened at some time although we may have altered them slightly and not used them in their entirety. I am always on the lookout for story ideas.'

In the very first series there was a storyline about Blue Watch rescuing a child's cat from a roof and then accidentally running over the hapless creature on their way out. This owed more than a little to the famous tale of how, during the 1977 firemen's strike, soldiers pressed into action in their Green Goddess trucks had rescued an old lady's cat from a tree. She was so grateful that she invited them in for a cup of tea but as they left her house, their Green Goddess ran over the cat.

Anita Bronson admits: 'Whenever we come to a new series of *London's Burning*, we go pale thinking how we're going to do it, simply because we cover so many storylines. It's a bit like *Hill Street Blues*. I once had ten plot lines all on the go at the same time. I was told that the viewers wouldn't be able to follow it but I was sure they would. People aren't cretins. They know if you just walk from A to B taking the dog out, you will see all sorts of things. And we do try to spring surprises with the characters.'

Anita's brother is a fireman but she did not use him as a tool of research. Instead she went to Euston Fire Station where she was greeted with male cries of 'Oh no, not another tart.' But she won them over and the men cooked her a special meal when she left and even bought her a lead for the stray puppy she picked up. She also spent a couple of nights at Peckham Fire Station in South London.

Anita discovered that many firemen lead double lives, doing other jobs to make ends meet. On the first training course, the cast were intrigued to meet one fireman who moonlighted by working for Gay Switchboard. 'I've met firemen selling insurance, doing computer maintenance,' she says. 'In *London's Burning*, we introduced Craig Fairbrass as Technique who did plumbing, body building and a bit of stripping on the side. In the series, he was being watched by the London Fire Brigade's secret "squirrels" who were videotaping absentees. In real life, the "squirrels" have now been disbanded.'

Multi-character drama is not easy to write. There are ten members of the Watch, plus assorted wives and girl-friends, and that's a lot of actors and actresses to cater for. It's no mean feat keeping them all happy with their storylines.

'There also has to be a sense of balance,' continues Anita Bronson. 'I'm always watching the balance of the show. I may feel we need an extra comedy element or something more powerful. With Colin, I thought we needed a young incredibly naive person who wanted to be a fireman. And he helped fill the comedy void left by the departure of Vaseline and Charisma. Greek Cypriot Nick Georgiadis was brought in as Station Officer as a contrast to his predecessor Tate. Whereas Tate was very paternal, Nick puts everybody on their toes. He stops

the show from becoming too cosy. Also there are lots of people from different ethnic minorities in the Fire Brigade so I felt it was important to bring in somebody who repre-sented a different strand of society. Nick's other quality is that he is very handsome so women viewers like him. If there's one thing I would like to do with *London's Burning*, it would be to bring in a second woman firefighter alongside Kate. I'd like to see the play-off between the two women.

'We're always hunting around for alternatives to fires. For this fifth series, we are doing a shoot around a huge motorway pile-up in fog, based on a number of motorway crashes'.

That particular episode provides a perfect example of the level of co-operation afforded to *London's Burning* by the emergency services. The Fire Brigade and the Motorway Police not only brought in a video of the actual news reports of a motorway crash but also a special video they had made simulating the pile-up using Matchbox toy vehicles – a sort of motorway madness in miniature.

Anita Bronson's favourite episodes were nine and ten in series four, the big warehouse fire. 'I had wanted to do a double episode for about two years – one that was almost entirely about a big shout. It was me who decided that Bayleaf and Hallam should be trapped. You choose people you think will have the greatest effect on the audience.'

A major consideration for the makers of *London's Burning* is how graphic the scenes should be. The hospital drama *Casualty* has been known to have grown men cowering behind the sofa but *London's Burning* has managed to avoid becoming too gruesome. 'It's a question of taste,' says Anita Bronson. 'You have to decide how much of a burning child you're going to show. It's very much a group decision. The last series went out at 8.45 in the evening and that made a big difference to us. We couldn't have anything much in the first 15 minutes until after the 9.00. watershed.'

David Humphries joined *London's Burning* in the third series. He had previously written episodes for *Minder, Hazell, Shoestring, Jemima Shore Investigates* and the controversial police show *Target*. Before writing his first script for *London's Burning*, he underwent the necessary research at Harrow Road Fire Station near Paddington. 'I spent a night watch and a day watch there and emerged full of admiration. I came to the conclusion that firefighters are a cross between nurses and the S.A.S!

'I just turned up in my jeans but they made me wear a uniform with jacket and boots. As we rushed to a shout, unbeknown to me, they handed me the Station Officer's jacket as a joke. So there I was supposedly a Station Officer in jeans! I got a lot of odd looks from some of the firefighters who weren't sure whether to approach me for orders. In the end, they thought better of it and decided I couldn't be for real'.

New to the writing team for the fifth series is the experienced Roger Marshall, the man responsible for some of the most spectacular episodes of *The Sweeney* as well as his own intriguing canal-boat drama *Travelling Man* starring Leigh Lawson. Marshall's research took him to Euston Fire Station for two days and two nights. 'Saturday night is usually their busiest night of the week but I think I must have been their talisman because when I was there, they didn't have a single fire to speak of. The nearest was a

kid throwing a burning mattress out of a window. Even so, I was left in no doubt that these people are genuine heroes.'

Once a draft script is written, Nobby Clark goes through it with a fine tooth-comb. He is the key man in ensuring that Fire Brigade procedures are adhered to on screen and that *London's Burning* looks authentic. Even relatively minor errors would immediately lead to a loss of credibility. 'My general job is to advise, correct the scripts and ensure that the portrayal of my profession is as good as we can get, working on the basis that it's warts and all and not a PR job. So when I receive the script, I highlight anything that is wrong. But it's no good me just saying, "That's wrong." I have to come up with an alternative. I do put my foot down. In the original film, there was a scene with food being thrown around at the station. You have to accept it, food does get thrown around but only very rarely. Then it came up in another script and I felt it was overplaying a rare occurrence. So I said, "No, we've shown that once. Let's move on."'

After the scripts have been written (subject to any last-minute re-writes of which there are plenty on *London's Burning*), the construction crews come in and re-build Colin Monk's Blackwall Fire Station if necessary. Last year it was left up as a permanent set at Jacob Street but in previous years it had been dismantled at the end of filming.

The heads of department then gather for the pre-planning stage. The designer starts work

'I never delude people about the horror of a television crew taking over their house,' says Location Manager Malcolm Treen. 'I always warn the householder: "You'll wonder what the hell's going on – there'll be lamps and cables everywhere. Above all, you'll be very glad when we have gone."'

Only the interior of Blackwall Fire Station exists as a permanent set at Jacob Street so any other regular locations have to be filmed elsewhere – in real houses. Thus the location managers have to persuade home-owners to allow the crew over their thresholds so that their property can become Sicknote's house, Hallam's house or Colin's mum's house.

'People whose houses we use are very understanding,' continues Malcolm Treen, 'which you've got to be. Having 80 people invade your house for a day is a bit off-putting even if you do get paid. Payments are made according to the length of stay and the amount of disruption. But we do make sure we tidy up afterwards – I like the house to be even tidier when we leave than when we arrive.

'Our stock locations include a couple of pubs just around the corner from Jacob Street – the Swan and Sugarloaf (known as the SAS) and the George. When we go to the George, we're able to film during opening hours because it has two bars. The regulars go in one bar and we film in the other. Hallam's house is in Peckham as is Nick's uncle's restaurant.

The only thing is it's supposed to be a Greek restaurant, but we film it all at a Turkish one!

'For Sicknote's house, we film at the Southwark home of cabbie Mick Nicholls and his wife Pat. While the storyline about Hallam's kitchen was running, we went filming to Sicknote's house one day, only to discover that Pat and Mick were having their kitchen done in real life. I thought, "Hang on, the kitchen's being done at Hallam's not Sicknote's." It was most confusing. Unknown to us, Pat and Mick had had an extension built on so we had to shorten it visually to make it look the same as it was.

So what does Pat Nicholls think of having her home taken over by a TV crew? 'Malcolm's right,' she sighs. 'It's chaos.'

There was no fun at the fair for Blue Watch.

along with the construction manager, the location managers, the directors and the production supervisor and his team.

The production supervisor is Chris Hall whose first task is to put together a crew. On *London's Burning*, the crew numbers around 70 but for a big fire scene, it can escalate to over 120.

Production designer Colin Monk scours the scripts to see what sets are needed. Colin's career began in the film industry as a member of the art department on movies such as The *Young Ones* with Cliff Richard and Billy Wilder's *The Private Life of Sherlock Holmes*. He then spent 16 years as a staff designer with LWT working on shows like *Agony, Me and My Girl* and *Child's Play* but not surprisingly he has never experienced anything quite like *London's Burning*. 'The main challenge *London's Burning* creates is actually dealing with fire. You can have a really nice set but when people want to burn it

Location manager, Kevin Holden, on the hot line.

down, it gives you other parameters to work in. Usually if there's a fire, we have to build a set because you can't go round burning people's houses down. You have to make a set that is fireproof but on which certain parts will burn. For sets we burn, we use a specially constructed "burn stage" at Jacob Street. It has a good chimney which lets out the fumes and things burn well there in a controlled environment.

'I've learned a lot from the Brigade about which materials to use in the construction of sets. In the early days, we used things like plasterboard because that dispersed the heat but it was really too heavy. There are plenty of materials coming on the market which we're trying out but at the moment I tend to favour tack clad. It not only disperses the heat but it's particularly good for that blistering effect you get in fires.

'Nobby and the Brigade used to help me by taking me out on real fires. I used their archives of photographs and talked with them with regard to how firefighters approached their work.

'That co-operation has been invaluable to me. It means that I've been to the aftermath of a few fires and so I have a much better idea of what the effects are. The room looks as if someone's hit it with a laser. You could move a cushion away and all the print of the fabric would still be there.

'Once I've got a material that contains the fire, the next thing I go for is the particular effect, like the wallpaper blistering. That may involve putting on several coats of lining paper with bumps underneath that have pockets of oil-based paint. Naturally we watch out for toxic materials but sometimes you need a little hint of it so that it gives you a different burn. Really my task is to try and achieve the right sort of effects without the set actually burning down and disappearing completely.'

All the materials used in making the sets are fire-resistant. They have to be in case of 're-takes'. There is not much point in the director going for another 'take' among a pile of ashes. And it would be rather expensive, not to mention time-consuming, to build it all over again. It is fair to say that they've learned from their mistakes.

Geoff Harrison, one of the two directors of photography, remembers the very first set that was built. 'It was for a fire at an Asian sweatshop. We built it with real materials and when we set fire to it, the whole thing went berserk. The set burned down. We lost it. The Fire Brigade put out the fire, checked it over and we all went home dejected. To make matters worse, the Brigade were called out twice in the night because the set had caught again. Although those long rolls of cloth which they use in dress-making were filled with water from the firemen's hoses, the heat was trapped inside and three hours later they caught fire. The reason the entire set had burned down was because although the set itself incorporated fire-resistant materials, the structure behind the set didn't. It got so hot in there that it went beyond the fire-resistant stuff. But we've learned from that and nowadays the structure of the set is held together with scaffolding.'

Working closely with Colin Monk is construction manager John Carman. Sometimes the sets are built by outside scenery contractors and then put up at Jacob Street by John's crew of three carpenters, two painters, a rigger and a stage-hand (plus freelances if necessary). 'Most of the sets have to be built in just 11 days,' says John Carman, 'and you're never sure what's going to be thrown at you. When we did a shout in a sewer, Colin designed this amazing 70ft. long sewer complete with manholes. It was made out of plywood and fibre glass and had to be built in two sections. We built the bottom half here and the top half went to the contractors. When it came back, it had to fit on perfectly so that you couldn't see the join. We put it on to the "burn stage" and we had no fewer than 1,700 gallons of water flowing through. And we didn't have a single leak.'

But things don't always go quite that smoothly. John remembers: 'When we did the episode where Vaseline was killed, when the lorry plunged into the water, we built a ramp that had to collapse. The lorry was driven on to the ramp and, for what seemed like 10 minutes to me but was probably only seven seconds, it didn't collapse. I didn't think it was going to. In the end, it did and it was perfect. But it's times like that when your heart stops beating because no matter how many of these you do, you're only remembered for the one that goes wrong.'

While interior shots are generally done at Jacob Street, there remains the question of where to film the exterior scenes. This is the province of location managers Malcolm Treen and Kevin Holden who handle alternate episodes. 'The script might call for an exterior warehouse fire,' says Malcolm Treen (who is accustomed to finding locations for the pranks on *Beadle's About*), 'and so I talk to the designer and draw up a list of likely venues. I also did *Dempsey and Makepeace* around South-East London so I know the area quite well.' The location manager then visits the possible settings, takes Polaroid photos and shows them to the director who considers each one carefully before settling on a short list of two or three. They go out again and once the director has made his final decision and the designer is happy, the location manager asks the owners of the premises for permission to film.

'Because *London's Burning* is so popular, most people are happy to let us film,' says Malcolm Treen. 'But when we tell people we want to burn their place, we do have to convince them it's not for real. It may look as if it's on fire but it's not.

'The simple things can be just as difficult to find locations for as fires and explosions. Last year we had an episode featuring a group of travellers on a piece of waste ground and their horse got stuck in the water. It sounded straightforward enough – all I needed was a pond, some grass and a few caravans scattered around. So I approached Southwark Council, who are terrifically helpful to us, and they said, "Yes, there's Burgess Park. You can dig a hole, fill it with water, put some caravans around it...but no horse because there's a bye-law against performing animals in the park."'

Eventually the council relented and gave their co-operation, but even filming a simple house scene can cause confusion. When *London's Burning* took over a house in Beckton, East London, for the day, they had to change the number from 55 to 31 to tally with the script. Since next door was also in vision, that too had to be changed from 57 to 33. Malcolm Treen says: 'All was fine until the postman came along, saw the new numbers and did a double-take. He was totally bemused, wondering what on earth to do with his pile of letters.'

The potentially alarming riot scene for Jack Rosenthal's film was mainly shot at the now demolished Redriff Estate in Rotherhithe, not far from the Jacob Street Studios. Even then the estate was only partly inhabited, mainly by retired dockers. With so many elderly people in the vicinity, it was essential that *London's Burning* allayed their fears and convinced them that it wasn't a genuine riot. So before filming, the production team threw a party for the residents to explain what would be happening.

Once permission is given, about a week before filming, there is a technical recce attended by the location manager, the director, his production assistant, the director of

Some people would choose the Bahamas, others the French Riviera but Property Buyer Will Hinton's idea of paradise is a day at a car breaker's yard in South-East London. For that's where he finds many of the vehicles which end up smashed and smouldering on London's Burning.

'It's all a matter of hunting around for the right vehicles at the right price,' says Will. 'The biggest problem for me is that whatever we do, we destroy. This means that I have to buy rather than hire, even with big lorries. After all, who wants a burned-out lorry back?

'Before any crash scene, I also have to arrange for the cars to be stripped because obviously you can't set fire to a car with a petrol tank. It would be too dangerous.'

Will has had some odd requests in his time. 'I once had to buy an interior of a submarine and I managed to track down this chap in Southampton who actually collects the insides of submarines. It's amazing what people have tucked away.

For an episode of Friday Night Live with Harry Enfield, I had to find an original Ovaltine card. There are only two left in the whole country but I was able to locate one of them. So you see the little things can be just as difficult as the Rolls-Royces.'

However Will was nearly moved to tears for an episode in the new series about young car thieves. 'The initial intention was to have these kids stealing Sierras but I said it would be more convincing if we used Porsches. So I went out and bought four Porsches for between £1,800 and £2,200 each but by the time we'd done them up and re-sprayed them, they looked like £15,000 cars. They were all T and X registrations but they looked wonderful. I must admit I wouldn't have minded one myself. So it was a real shame to see them burn, particularly because the people who had owned them had taken so much care of them. Still, we might be able to sell some of the parts that aren't too damaged for salvage.'

James Hazeldine (Bayleaf) turns director for an episode in series five.

photography, the designer, the lighting director and property master at which the director explains how he wants to shoot the scene. And the next time they go back, it's for real – well, television.

By now the main cast have assembled. Each year a few weeks before filming, they're sent off to a Fire Brigade Training Course organised by Nobby Clark. This not only applies to new members of the cast – even the established hands go. On their return, there is a readthrough of as many scripts as are available. The aim is to have four or five written before filming commences. Although it is a television series, *London's Burning* works more like a film. There are no weeks of rehearsal, the actors just go straight into filming – a camera rehearsal and then a 'take'. If a couple of the cast want to practise a scene more thoroughly, they usually go through their lines in a spare office around the Jacob Street complex.

Of course there are also numerous minor characters to be cast in each episode like Second Lady On Bus or Spotty Youth. For casting director Corinne Rodriguez, these two-line parts are often the hardest to fill. 'As much as anything, it's so time-consuming,' says Corinne, 'because there have been literally hundreds of these little walk-on roles.'

In keeping with his team philosophy, producer Paul Knight likes to keep the same directors on *London's Burning*. 'Gerry Mill and John Reardon have been with us from the start while Keith Washington joined us two years ago. And James Hazeldine, who plays Bayleaf, has directed an episode of the fifth series. The thing is that these guys are all familiar with the show. They understand how it works. And that is so important.'

Come filming day, production supervisor Chris Hall and production co-ordinator Jenny Brassett will have sorted out precisely what camera and lighting equipment is required for the shoot. Every day a call sheet, written by the second assistant director, is issued to check that everything will be in the right place at the right time. The two Blackwall appliances are now owned by LWT but were originally on loan from the London Fire Brigade's spare fleet. Because they were spares, the number of appliances used by real firefighters always remained the same – *London's Burning* didn't reduce the fleet by one iota. Things like ladders are loaned from the LFB as and when required. The programme also gets equipment from other Brigades, which is then rebadged to look like a London brigade's. Additional essential items to be arranged on filming days are transport to and from location and, arguably most vital of all, location catering.

Every evening at the end of the day's filming, the laboratory picks up that day's rushes and sound rushes and processes them overnight. The sound tapes are transferred the following morning and its all then brought back to Jacob Street where it comes under the scrutiny of supervising editor Frank Webb.

Producer Paul Knight (right) joins filming on location.

'I view the rushes on a Steenbeck which is a flat projector for viewing and editing,' explains Webb from his compact Portakabin. 'The Steenbeck has two sound tracks so I can lay in music and extra dialogue. When the rushes come to me after being developed, the first thing that happens is they are married up ("sunk up" as we call it) with the sound track. Then in the evening I sit down with the director and we look at them and discuss them. Next I cut the film as I think best and then the director will come back and we'll go through it again. He might ask for certain shots to be put back or suggest others be taken out, bearing in mind that for a 60-minute episode, the running time is only actually 52 minutes to allow for commercial breaks. When we're both happy with the end result, we call in Paul Knight.

'When we're satisfied with the picture, we start on the sound. I go through it with Nobby Clark. I might find a section where I think we're a bit flat for sound and I'll suggest he gets a few lines of dialogue written there just to brighten the thing up. Then I get in our dubbing editors, who work on sound only, and I might ask for something like the sound of a car to be inserted, again to make sure there is something happening in the background. The titles are added and composer Simon Brint will come in and go through it with the director to decide where the incidental music should go.

Simon Brint's name and face will be familiar to fans of early *French and Saunders* series as he and alternative comedian Rowland Rivron comprised the unlikely musical duo Raw Sex. Indeed, together with Roddy Matthews, Brint and Rivron composed the title-music for *London's Burning*.

Frank Webb sums up: 'We then mix it all together and the result is what you see on screen. We really do edit as we go along – the whole process of editing and dubbing takes about three months.'

London's Burning is ready for its 19 million fans.

As the Fire Brigade's official advisor, it was down to Nobby Clark to obtain the equipment and also to write a training course for the actors. 'I think the training course was the best investment LWT made,' he says. 'Before the original Jack Rosenthal film, I said that if the actors are going to play firefighters, they need to know what they are doing. So I arranged for a two-week course for the whole of Blue Watch at the London Fire Brigade Training Centre at Southwark where they learned how to handle hose, climb ladders correctly, use the breathing apparatus and go through the dreaded rat run. We also had them practising how to slide down a pole properly. On the very first day Jerome Flynn, who played he-man Rambo, came down the pole for the first time, fell at the bottom and hit his knee on a pipe. There I was after just one hour of training and my first dealings with the cast were Rambo with a swollen knee. I thought, "My God, what have I let myself in for? I've injured an actor already!"

'The cast now go for a refresher course before each series. It has been slightly modified for the actors – we're not looking for the same standard but the dangers are the same and the equipment is the same weight and size. The actors have to be made aware of things like how to hold a jet, because, if you let go of a jet, it can snake around all over the place and break someone's leg. After training, all of the cast are sent to a different operational station for one or two nights so that they get a flavour of the Fire Brigade.'

3 PLAYING WITH FIRE

Nobody on *London's Burning* will ever forget the terrifying moment when they came face to face with a flashover, the type of racing ball of fire which caused such carnage in the King's Cross Underground Station inferno of 1987, killing 31 people, among them a fire officer. The *London's Burning* flashover happened in 1989 while filming a fire sequence for the fifth episode of series two. It was caused by a build-up of hot gases in the set and as the gases burned off, a flashover occurred.

The director on that episode was the experienced Gerry Mill, one of our most accomplished television practitioners. His work includes *Robin of Sherwood* (produced by Paul Knight), *Holding On* and *Yellowthread Street*. He recalls: 'We had learned very quickly on London's Burning that for shooting fire scenes the thing to do was build a set, not burn a real building, because that way we could take out walls and put cameras where we wanted them. Once you set fire to things, that rather dictates where you go. So for this particular scene we built a two-storeyed set and our firefighters had to burst in from the ground floor, come charging up the staircase with a hosepipe and get to the landing where there was an old man and his dog trapped in the bedroom.

'It was all carefully planned with cameras looking in from all angles, even up traps, but it meant that we had to build the top floor on a huge rostrum about 12 ft high. We'd worked it all out – we had the actors off set and there was the usual standby crew with hosepipes in case things got out of hand. All our fires come from propane gas jets with totally controllable flames which can go up and down and on and off whenever we want them to. When I call "Cut!", the flames go out.

'We were at the top of the stairs, we lit all the flames which are all numbered and I was shouting, "Up on number one, up on number two." I thought if you're coming up a blazing staircase, it's got to look good. If it looks weedy, there's no point in turning the water on. So I was saying, "We need more – it must look dangerous."

'The next thing we'd got a flashover. This fireball came flying up the stairs and ripped across the ceiling. It was so hot and so quick. It came at us in about a tenth of a second. It takes all the air out of your lungs. You can't shout, "Run for it" or "Cut!". You just inhale and your brain stops.

'People were singed and burned but thankfully nothing too serious. I dived through a window to get down below and as I jumped, the curtains wrapped themselves around my ankles. So I was hanging upside down outside this window!

'It was scary though. We took a tea break for about an hour and calmed down. We went back and this time we took the roof off the set so that when we lit it, the flames went straight up.'

The cast were watching events from the outside. 'Mercifully the flashover happened before we went in,' says Rupert Baker. 'It was a very narrow stairwell which we would have been working up and the fire went all the way through it. Everybody scrambled out. But if we had been in that stairwell, it would have been quite nasty.'

Gerry Mill adds: 'I did an attic fire for the new series and that got out of control in precisely the same way. But we were more aware this time, we had even more firemen standing by than before. What happened was we were shooting an interior scene and we had blackout curtains draped outside so as not to let daylight into the attic. But the heat was so intense that these blackout drapes just caught fire and melted and came straight down on people. Again there were just a few singes but it could have been much worse.'

Thankfully such incidents are few and far between on *London's Burning*. Considering they are literally playing with fire, they have an excellent safety record. For make no

mistake, the blazes may be on tap and controllable but the flames are real and very hot. Nobody connected with the show is allowed to treat fire lightly.

For potentially hazardous fire scenes, the actors make way for real off-duty firefighters. Even though they are trained, it is pointless to risk the cast in such situations, particularly since viewers at home would be unable to see their faces anyway through the masks which they wear as part of the compulsory breathing apparatus. In addition, there is always a real fire crew in attendance to act as safety cover.

As with many things on *London's Burning*, safety is down to Nobby Clark. 'If it's something on safety, I have the power of veto. I know where the buck stops and in the past I have halted filming. With so much involved, you have to be accountable and the crew know I'm not going to cry wolf too often but safety must come first.

'I helped advise with the construction of the sets which go on the "burn stage". They have to be fire-resistant. I also check each set with designer Colin Monk to make sure there are enough exits for the various personnel and, in the case of a two-storey set, that there is emergency lighting on the staircases to get people away.

'One thing the flashover taught us was that we didn't have sufficient vents on the sets. Now we have more vents to allow the gases to escape.

'You also have to be aware of how long the actors are wearing breathing apparatus because you know how much it weighs. The cast have coped with the fire scenes very well. I think the Brigade would actually have employed three of them. Hopefully our fires are always safe so you don't know whether their bottle would go in a real situation but we have given them a few hairy experiences.'

A way in which the risk on a fire set is minimised is by keeping crew numbers to a minimum. Only essential personnel are allowed in the vicinity of the blaze. And they are fully protected. The camera operator, director of photography, focus puller, sound boom operator and Nobby Clark alongside them as safety officer, all wear Brigade breathing apparatus. Naturally those fighting the fire, whether they be actors or real firemen, wear the standard Brigade fire-proof clothing.

But, as Colin Monk points out, 'Although the camera ops wear breathing apparatus, there are still make-up people, electricians and so on who have to be nearby so you have to keep them safe too. It is very dangerous because even though we are doing it in a controlled way, fire is fire and it can run riot.

'My concern doesn't end with the fire being put out. Within the design aspect, I have to cater for water. After extinguishing the flames with their hoses, our standby crew will clear the surplus water away but you're still left with a saturated set. If you've got to do another "take", you have to build lots of contingencies into the set design to cater for any eventuality. I try to build the majority of my sets off the ground so that I've got an escape route for the water. And of course I need escape routes for personnel so that if something did go wrong, I could let the set burn down and nobody would be hurt. Safety is always our prime consideration. Our track record is very good but you do have to have eyes in the back of your head.'

To avoid creating toxic gases on set when burning furniture, plastics are kept down to a minimum. If a burned-out sofa is being shown, they don't burn it on the set. Instead they burn it elsewhere and then create smoke and steam to put around it to create the same effect.

So how do they achieve such spectacular fires on *London's Burning*? Special effects supervisor Tom Harris explains: 'The principle of fire effects is to make it as safe as possible and then make it look as dangerous as possible. We use a piece of equipment called a woofer filled with propane gas and set at a certain pressure. This gives a controlled ball of flame. A house may look on fire but it's really just a number of gas jets which can be switched on or off and can go up and down. When the director shouts "Cut!", everything goes out.'

The propane gas gives a very visual effect, so much so that the fires on *London's Burning* often look better than the real thing. But there is one notable difference. Whereas real firefighters are trained to put out fires, on *London's Burning* they are told to deliberately miss the source of the fire. 'They have to aim their hoses to miss,' confesses Nobby Clark. 'Otherwise we would lose the effect. So it is a total cheat.'

Quite simply, the fire has to be kept going for as long as possible to allow the director to get the shots he requires. Gerry Mill says: 'As a director, you need all you can get. You need all manner of shots and angles – you have to shoot far more material than you actually use. With some of the little flat fires we do, they can actually come in with a sprinkler hose and put it out in ten seconds. That's useless to me. So I keep the effect going. Our firefighters will put out an armchair and turn round and I'll say, "Up with that again." So the flames re-appear and they complain, "I just put that out."'

Of course there's no fire without smoke and that presents one of the team's biggest problems. In real life, most fires produce clouds of black smoke. 'That's the one thing we can't do,' says Gerry Mill. 'In the early days, we would film and all we would see was a black screen. Nothing else. It was hopeless. So we have to use grey smoke instead. The

Fire Brigade told us that it wasn't realistic but now they accept it. The other thing is that black smoke is lethal. In a fire, it's not the flames that get you, it's the smoke. Four good lungfulls of toxic smoke and you're dead. You don't worry about the flames after that! Black smoke is also cancerous. And just because you're making a television programme, doesn't make you immune.'

Like the flames, the smoke is on tap and comes courtesy of a smoke machine. The amount can be increased or decreased as required. Each set has a vent in the ceiling so the set is filled with smoke and then the vent is opened to allow any surplus to escape.

For it is one thing being able to create a fire but another thing making it look good on screen. Nobby Clark says: 'I like to see a fire sequence that is like a Giles cartoon. Apart from the obvious dialogue and up-front action, I like there to be bits and pieces going on in the background. The more you look into it, the more you see. For me, that makes it feel real.'

This is where the director of photography comes in. There are two on *London's Burning* – Paul Bond and Geoff Harrison. Their principal task is to light the scene, to make sure that it conveys the necessary drama into the living rooms of the nation. With the vast majority of television programmes, lighting comes courtesy of powerful lamps but here again, at least in fire scenes, *London's Burning* strays from the norm. Lamps would simply be unable to stand the heat of a prolonged fire scene and if they were placed far enough away so as not to melt, the amount of light they would generate would be woefully inadequate for the requirements of television. Besides there is often sufficient light generated by the flames themselves. And no artificial lighting can compare with that of a real flame. However there will always be pockets of darkness where a little extra lighting is required so Tom Harris and his special effects team have developed small hand-held triangular-shaped flame bars known as fishtails. Butane gas is fed through a metal fishtail to produce neat little flames.

Paul Bond says: 'The fishtails are an enormous help to us. We use them like torches. The beauty of them is that we can move them around the set and place them wherever

Director of photography, Paul Bond, lights a scene with a specially-developed flame bar.

we want them in exactly the same way that you use photographic lamps. I like to carry them around and light a face or wave one under the camera so that you get a little flick of flame and a 3-D effect. It means that we're able to get the right colour and the right flicker from the flames themselves. It would be difficult to achieve that effect artificially. Where it looks best is when the firefighters are wearing face masks and the fire you're lighting with reflects in the face mask. It's very visual and very pretty.'

Geoff Harrison adds: 'You simply can't beat real flames. Lighting effects are somehow never the same – they look too much like disco lighting. If we have conventional lights on a set that's going to burn, they go in the first three or four seconds. They just explode with the heat. Having said that, a fluorescent tube exploding does make nice pictures.'

Nobody on *London's Burning* ever rests on their laurels. They are constantly looking for ways of improving their technique when it comes to shooting fires and other major incidents. The introduction of fishtails is one example – another is the development of the apparatus worn by the camera operator Ken Lowe.

'We are able to put the camera and, more importantly, the camera operator into the actual fire,' says Paul Bond. 'The first thing we had to do was clad the camera as best we could so that it's proofed against the heat. It's nice for us to get shots of fires being fought with hoses which splash all over the place so we have a revolving glass disc which spins round in front of the camera lens and flings off the water. That way, we can see through at the fire being fought without having all those drops of water on the lens. We then discovered that as soon as you had water and the heat of the flame, you had steam everywhere. On the very first fire we did, the flames were good, the smoke was right, we put the camera in and it was great. Then we put a hose in and suddenly the place filled with steam and we couldn't photograph anything. The whole thing was wiped out. I think we had about three seconds of film in that first fire. So we introduced a hoseline of air that comes in and blows air on to our spinning disc, thereby blowing away the condensation and preventing the lens from misting up. Then we found that there were further problems if the air was too cold. So there's now a heater in the air line too. It really is the most complicated piece of equipment.

'When we're doing an interior fire, we wear the same breathing apparatus that firefighters wear. But the camera operator doesn't wear a helmet and can't have a full face mask because he's got to put his eye to the camera. So Ken Lowe has a one-eyed

MAKE-UP

'Many nights I'm at home making blood.' No, these are not the words of Dracula's assistant or the gruesome Hannibal Lecter but of Roseann Samuel, the make-up supervisor on *London's Burning*.

Roseann talks with great enthusiasm about blood. 'There are lots of different types of blood like wet blood and congealed blood and the colours vary depending on where you're bleeding from.' With the number of victims on the show, Roseann is kept constantly busy which is why she can often be found experimenting at home making her own blood from a recipe of maple syrup, cochineal and liquidised redcurrant jelly. If there isn't sufficient time to concoct her own brew, she uses one of the proprietary brands of stage blood.

'For burns, we use a lot of gelatine mixtures and professional products like tuplast. As guidance, I use photographs from the Burns Unit at Roehampton Hospital and also from the Fire Brigade, taken at actual incidents. Full head wounds are usually achieved with the help of clingfilm. We put surgical adhesive all over the head and then dry that off so it's just tacky. Then we put clingfilm on and move it around a little so it actually looks taut and you get the effect of muscle and tendon. Then we add on lots of different colours – black if the victim has been burned to death.

'When we did the guy trapped under the tube train, I ordered a set of crushed legs from the canteen! I had the caterers boil me up some lamb bones and then I crushed

them up and made wounds out of gelatine. The poor chap's leg wound was made from gelatine and glycerine and built up with cotton wool. Then I put the bones and some fresh lamb meat into the centre of the wound and added fake wet blood. The effect was great, especially with the lamb bone sticking out!'

Roseann won a BAFTA Award for Best Television Make-Up for her work on Agatha Christie's Poirot. 'As part of my duties, I was responsible for Poirot's famous waxed moustache. David Suchet, who played *Poirot*, had a new one each episode. During filming, it used to go on David in the morning, come off at lunchtime and be pinned up for safe keeping before going back on for the afternoon. I had to keep it in immaculate condition.'

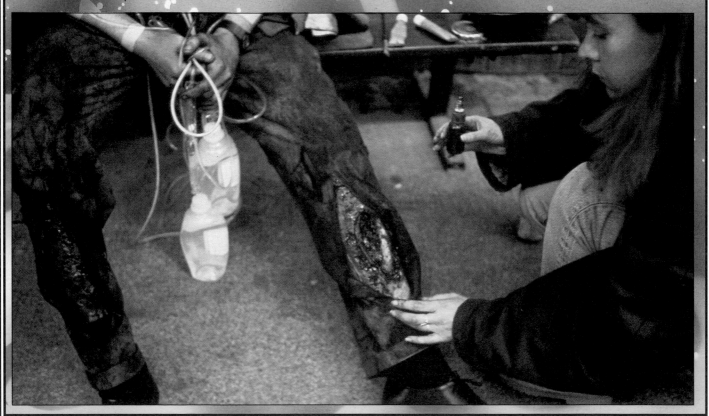

mask, his focus eye being protected by the camera itself. Also he can't wear an air bottle on his back like real firefighters. He's already got the weight of the camera and to have a heavy bottle as well would simply be too cumbersome. So he has a line to a bottle which an assistant carries for him.'

Geoff Harrison, another stalwart of *Dempsey and Makepeace*, worked on the original Jack Rosenthal film. That was the start of his education in shooting fire. 'We watched a lot of news footage of fires and also the Fire Brigade's own footage because they have a video unit which they send in to as many incidents as they can. They use the video as a record and also to analyse the event afterwards and discuss which way they fought it and how they beat the fire. All of that was invaluable to us. We spent a month studying that and newsreels of the Broadwater Farm riots. We tried to make our filming as close to the real footage as we could so that you weren't sure whether it was real or fabricated.

'That's been the ambition since then on *London's Burning*. We play the domestics as very straightforward, stylised film and then when we go into a shout, it's the opposite. We go with hand-held cameras for that documentary look. It's intentionally scruffy – I even trip the camera operator up every now and again or give him a subtle nudge so that the angle slips.

Along with the director himself, the director of photography is the one who will order more flame or more smoke for a particular scene. Geoff Harrison has been working on *London's Burning* for six years now but even he confesses that for all the know-how he has acquired over that period and despite all the detailed planning that goes into the preparation of a fire scene, once it starts he can never be exactly sure what the outcome will be.

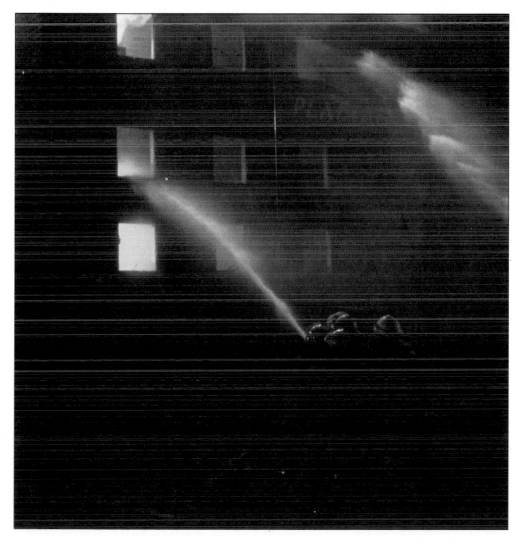

'Once a flame gets going and starts to burn, you don't really know what is going to happen. You think something's going to be really dangerous and nothing happens at all. Then the next one you do, there will be a little pocket in a corner which runs out of oxygen. So it fills with gas. As it fills, it's no problem until the gas slips round that corner and meets oxygen. Then it explodes and you've suddenly got a fireball – a 4ft ball of flame rolling along the ceiling. But you don't know that until it actually happens. Our extra vents should prevent these flashovers – in fact we even create our own flashovers now – but it's still a risky business. Nobby tells us how big he thinks the flames are going to be but when it comes down to it, you're 20ft away and you suddenly feel the hairs on your face burning because you're too close.

'Although it's a dangerous series to do, nobody wants to say no. People like camera operator Ken Lowe won't refuse to do anything so it's up to Paul and I not to push them too far. I remember one episode we did with a hospital fire. Most of it was done on the "burn stage" at Jacob Street but we couldn't create anything big enough so we had to do some filming at St James's Hospital, Wandsworth. It was due for demolition, and indeed has since been knocked down, which is why we were allowed to use it.

'It all got too hot too quickly. We had three cameras and on the one at the highest level, the rubber hood around the camera melted within five seconds. And on that occasion a real firefighter, who was standing in for our actors, got his hand burned. This guy was happily fighting the fire and it was a great shot. We were saying, "Go to the left a bit. A bit further. Great. Carry on." What we didn't realise was that his hand was actually in the fire. He had a glove on but his hand was burning and he came out all blistered. He simply hadn't wanted to say no.'

On *London's Burning*, although they have undergone their two weeks' training, the actors are naturally not expected to carry out every duty of a real firefighter. In the most treacherous situations, a stunt man or a genuine firefighter will take over. But that is not to say that the cast don't fight fires. They get well and truly stuck in to the smaller blazes and, even on the big shouts, they will douse the flames in the less confined areas, often alongside a real firefighter. The off-duty firefighters, employed as extras, used to put out most of the blazes but as the actors have grown to master the vagaries of hoses and ladders, they are doing more and more themselves.

One of the director's most difficult tasks on the series is to show the viewing public that it is a real actor fighting the fire and not just a double. Two factors make this more awkward. Firstly, in fires the actors must wear full breathing apparatus including a helmet and face mask which renders identification virtually impossible. Secondly, because flames look more spectacular against a dark background, most of the fire scenes are filmed at night.

'It's our biggest problem proving to people that it's our guys actually doing it,' says director Gerry Mill. 'We have to get in really close either with a fishtail or a torch and shine it on their faces so that the people at home can see that it really is an actor. We hand-hold the cameras because we need to be mobile in case things catch fire and fall. Sometimes we have to get out of the way pretty smartly. We usually run two cameras and you just watch for what ignites well and who gets what and you chase them. Say Kate is fighting a nice blazing table, you go on her. The director of photography will say, "Quick, bring me a flame" and you see a big close-up and you see it's her. Then the viewers know that Sam Beckinsale is in there fighting that fire.'

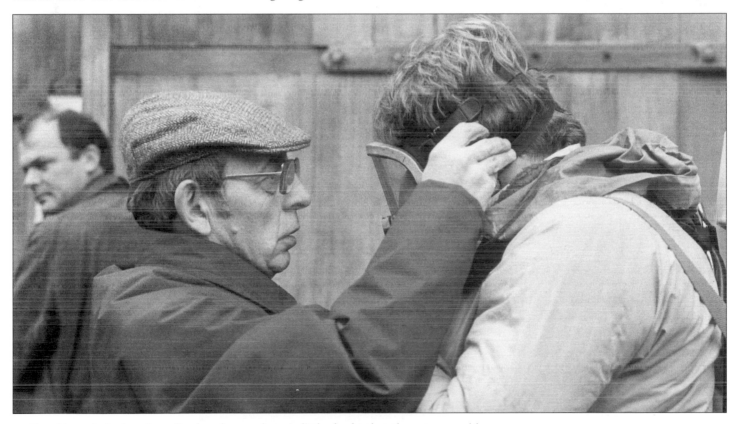

Should a relatively minor fire break out, there is little doubt that the actors could put it out without any outside help. In a way, they would probably find it easier because they would actually be allowed to extinguish the flames instead of having to aim their hoses to miss as they do with the controlled propane gas flames. Indeed back on the original film when a garage blaze went a little too far, the cast did put it out. It was only intended to be a short scene but the cameras continued to roll for the half-hour or so while the actors fought it in case action inserts were needed for the future. 'It was great experience to be able to do it ourselves,' says Rupert Baker. 'Our biggest problem was that with the cameras rolling, we had to remember that it wasn't just like the training course – we had to call each other by our character names. It was no use shouting to Gerard Horan, "Give me some more hose, Gerard." It had to be "Give me some more hose, Charisma."'

Over she goes – the spectacular coach crash.

The enormous success of *London's Burning* is due in no small part to the spectacular stunts that seem to occur on a weekly basis. We have seen dramatic shots of human torches, a coach full of children somersaulting down a bank and a luxury boat exploding in a packed marina, to name but a few. The stunt co-ordinator on *London's Burning* is the vastly experienced Alf Joint who started out doing film stunts some 30 years ago. 'Basically, my job on this series is to make sure the stunts work. Sure, I've gone in and skidded the odd car but principally mine is a non-active role.

'My involvement with *London's Burning* begins at the planning stage. I go through the script with producer Paul Knight who is very good at suggesting stunt ideas. Our aim is to put the firefighters in jeopardy on screen. I have to get the right stuntman for the job and so it is up to me to know the best drivers, the best fallers and so on. For the new series, we did a 150ft fall from a crane. Not a lot of people do a fall well. They might fall off like a piece of dead meat or do a half-hearted somersault that looks phoney. So I enlisted the help of Dave Bickers, the former motor-cross champion. He's got a thing called a fan descender which first came into operation as a safe method of training airborne troops. It is essentially a long length of cable wrapped around a cylinder with a rotating fan on the end of the cylinder. Normally as the body drops, it picks up speed but the rotating fan actually slows the descent. And because the faller is wearing a full body harness, he can mime the fall beautifully and topple over from head to toe.'

Few stunts on *London's Burning* have been more ambitious than that to turn over a 10-ton fire appliance. Special effects maestro Tom Harris reveals how it was done. 'The thing with fire engines is that they are designed not to turn over. We checked with the manufacturers, Dennis, and they informed us that an engine had to tilt through 47 degrees in order to go over. So we had to alter the complete structure of it. Normally the water tanks on the appliance are at the bottom so we moved them to the top to make it more unstable.'

The director on that episode was Les Blair. The stunt was very dramatic and had everyone holding their breath. Gerry Mill remembers: 'We turned the thing over by using a big ramp and had eight cameras going... it was superb. The windscreen went brilliantly and we had one camera on the road and the engine slid along the road on its side towards this camera. There's no knowing when 10 tons of fire engine is going to stop but luckily it ground to a halt just 5ft short of the camera.'

Another piece of equipment that is used a lot on stunts is a gun-like mechanism known as a nitrogen ram. This is more powerful than a simple ramp and can actually turn heavy vehicles right over rather than just on their side. But it can also be used on humans. Alf Joint explains: 'It's like compressed air but with nitrogen instead and fires a wooden shell held in by wire. As it is fired, the recoil from the ram projects you into the air. It operates on the same principle as the circus cannon that fires the lady into the net and is used all the time for explosions in war films, for one-foot and two-foot take-off. We got one in for a scene in which a guy was catapulted through the air by an explosion as he opened a garage door. Stuntman Gabe Cronnelly stood on the ram and it was timed so that as the flames came out of the garage, the ram would explode and Gabe would be blown back through the air. It works really well.'

Gabe Cronnelly and the nitrogen ram were also employed for the dramatic coach crash in series four. The script involved a complicated sequence in which a coach packed with youngsters on half-term holiday had just emerged from the Blackwall Tunnel when the kids started mucking about. The driver, distracted by their antics, swerved to avoid a car and ploughed through the central barrier into a cement lorry. The lorry driver scrambled out but was hit by a car which in turn crashed into the coach and burst into flames. The coach was meant to roll down an embankment and come to a halt with all the children still trapped inside. Blue Watch were then supposed to cut a hole in the coach to get them out.

Coaches are built not to turn over so the powerful recoil from the firing of the nitrogen ram was used to lift one side of the coach off the ground and help it on its way. The ram was placed upside down beneath the coach and as it was fired into the ground, the vehicle would go over. So Cronnelly had to drive the coach along the road, hit a precise mark, pull a lever that would fire the shell into the ground thereby turning the coach over and then steer the vehicle over the side and down the bank. There was no possibility of filming such a sequence on a public road so eventually the team found a stretch of tarmac at Chertsey in Surrey, that had been used for tank research. Not only was it off the beaten track, it also had the required 40ft drop, down which the coach was supposed to tumble.

As with all the stunts on *London's Burning* it was carefully plotted. Director John Reardon, a long-standing director with LWT including such popular shows as *Agony*, *Me and My Girl*, *Whoops Apocalypse* (for which he won a Royal Television Society Award as Best Director) and *The Gentle Touch*, takes up the story. 'We bought two identical coaches and converted the one which was to crash to incorporate a special cage in which the stuntman would be strapped to avoid being killed. The child occupants of that doomed coach were actually cardboard cut-outs. The other coach was left intact and filled with real children. We drove them around an estate and inside the coach we simply spun the camera round and got the children to jump from side to side. That way, it looked as if the coach was turning over and the children were involved in the crash.

'We had seven cameras trained on the crashing coach. We rehearsed it for an hour and a half and built a series of safety banks. We sat and talked about whether we should be giving the impression that children were hurt. But for me the thing that would really get to the audience more than anything else was the fact that children were in jeopardy.

All concerned were full of praise for the children who were then placed in the wrecked coach. Samantha Beckinsale, who plays Kate, remembers: 'I was using a pneumatic saw to cut a hole in metal just three inches from one girl's hand and she didn't flinch a bit.'

The stunt men usually fly through the air with the greatest of ease – thanks to a trampoline.

The coach crash was enormously impressive visually, helped by the fact that stunt co-ordinator Alf Joint is always on the lookout for ways to liven things up. 'If I see there's a problem anywhere, I'll pep it up. With the coach crash, we had two cars – one missing the cement lorry, the other one hitting it – and then I realised that all the other cars were stopping neatly behind which in reality they just wouldn't do. So I put myself in a car and skidded across broadside to make it better visually.'

Among the most spectacular stunts on *London's Burning* are the human torches. Even with the recession, there aren't too many actors around who are willing to set fire to themselves so stuntmen take their place. Again every precaution is taken to ensure that no matter how horrifying the situation may look on screen, in reality it is controlled and as safe as possible.

'Protective clothing is obviously all important,' explains Alf Joint. 'The stuntman wears flame-proof Nomex underwear (the sort worn by motor racing drivers) then a flame-proof silver suit which reflects the heat. On top of that he wears fire-proof clothing – it has to be otherwise it would melt away to reveal the silver suit underneath. The head is usually wrapped in a Nomex balaclava beneath which is fitted an air-pipe leading to a small oxygen cylinder, rather like a mini aqualung, strapped under the clothing. Then Zellgel is applied. Zellgel is a bit like wallpaper

paste and has to be kept refrigerated. And that's put on all the exposed areas like the face and hands. It can stand a flame for eight seconds. Then a paraffin-based jelly is plastered all over the body and ignited with a match. Although the suit is fire-proof, you can't go on too long because what happens is you start to sweat with the heat, your body sweat boils and that scalds you inside.'

To Alf, stunts are all in a day's work, not much different from going to the office. He even refers to them as 'gags' but he is of course only too aware that they're no laughing matter, especially when they go wrong.

'When you're doing fire stunts in a confined space, you have to remember to get everybody of the way. You also have to guard against complacency – it's when you get over-confident that things go wrong. Touch wood, we've had very few mishaps. One that did get a bit nasty was for a shout on board a ship in which the engineer was blasted by an almighty explosion. Tim Lawrence was my stunt engineer and the idea was that he would open a door and a wall of flame would come at him. To give the impression that he was being blown up by the explosion, we had a little 3ft square trampoline. He was supposed to stand astride it, then jump on to it and throw himself backwards through the air. We rehearsed it thoroughly but unfortunately when we did the "take" he jumped forward on to the trampoline instead of backwards. It's very difficult to counteract a

STUNT CO-ORDINATOR

Looking at the solid frame of silver-haired Stunt Co-Ordinator Alf Joint, with the best will in the world it is hard to imagine that he once doubled for actress Lee Remick! 'I doubled for Lee on the 1976 film *The Omen*. I did a fall when she was pushed out of a hospital window.'

Lee Remick is just one of a number of movie stars who have had 59-year-old Alf as their stunt double. 'I used to double for Richard Burton a lot, on films like *Where Eagles Dare*, because I looked like him in those days. I also doubled for Marlon Brando on *Superman* as well as Rod Steiger and Kirk Douglas.'

Alf started out in showbusiness doing a trampoline and bar act but then his partner broke his neck. Alf went on to do summer seasons at Pontin's holiday camps until the producers of the 1963 Viking epic *The Long Ships* (starring Sidney Poitier and Richard Widmark) wanted somebody to do a 90 ft dive. Somebody mentioned Alf's name and that dive filmed in Yugoslavia was the beginning of a long and fruitful association with the movie industry. He went on to help with the flying scenes on three of the Superman films and also worked on such box office hits as *An American Werewolf in London* and *Kelly's Heroes*.

'One of the things I like about *London's Burning* is that the shouts are based on true stories. Even the one where the chap got a curtain ring wedged on his private parts was based on a real incident in Lancashire except there it was a pair of scissors that got stuck. Apparently the firemen asked him, "How did you do that?" And he said, "It wasn't easy..."'

forward motion and then go backwards and instead of going back, he went straight up and the fire hit him in the face, burning the inside of his nose and mouth.'

The standby firefighters, who are always armed with wet towels on such occasions, rushed in to cover Tim's burns. He was taken to Guy's Hospital with concussion and second degree burns and was kept in overnight for observation. 'The burns looked worse than they were,' states Tim, 'but the doctors said they had learned from the Piper Alpha and King's Cross disasters that people could inhale flame without knowing it and that could cause trouble with their breathing. It was just one of those things – I knew something was amiss when I hit the mat with my cheeks burning and lips stinging.'

The type of miniature trampoline used in the ship explosion is commonplace in stunt work. On an early episode of *London's Burning*, a lonely widow, deliberately trying to get herself run over, was seen being hurled over the bonnet of a car on impact. That effect was achieved by bouncing a stuntman, dressed as the old lady, off the stationary car with the aid of a trampoline. In the third series when new recruit Colin, wearing full breathing apparatus, inadvertently put his hose on a junction box and was blown back through the air, knocking down two firefighters in the process, the trampoline again played a vital part.

Alf Joint describes how that scene was done. 'Colin's stunt double stood on a teeter board, which is a bit like an old see-saw. We had one shot of him going back from the teeter board out of shot, then we did another one of him going further back off a mini trampoline. Finally we did a third shot outside on the mini trampoline of him hitting the firemen and knocking them to the ground. We cut the three together and it all worked as one shot.'

One person who doesn't always share Alf Joint's enthusiasm for stunts – especially human torches – is director Gerry Mill. 'I don't like doing human torch episodes,' he admits. 'I did one for an episode in a café where the owner set fire to himself by mistake.

'My one worry about stunts, particularly fire stunts, is you set it all up, you know you've got good people, and you stand back and say, "If you could scream while you're

doing it..." All you see is flailing arms and this man screaming and you think, "If it's gone wrong and he's actually screaming for help, how do we know?"

'For this scene, I was outside in the street looking in at the dark cafe because I thought the best shot was one where you see a bit of flame and then you see the figure coming at you. The last thing I said to Peter Diamond beforehand was, "When you throw the stool through the window, the minute you've hit the glass, that's a cut. I won't go on from there. You can hit the deck and they'll put you out."

'I shouted, "Action" and this flailing figure came roaring at us, flames everywhere, he threw the stool and I shouted, "Cut." You always rush in after a stunt to make sure the guy's all right but when I looked into this dark café, there was nobody there. He'd gone. And there was just that moment when you think, "Christ, what's happened to him?" What had happened was in the darkness, Nobby Clark and Co. had got in, wrapped him in the blanket and dragged him out the back because his air pipe had come off. He'd lost his air supply. He was actually burning up inside. He was terribly hot and severely distressed. The poor guy was in a really bad way.'

Producer Paul Knight and the writers are constantly trying to bring a greater variety of incidents into *London's Burning*. A firefighter's life is not only about fighting fires – the Brigade have to deal with all manner of rescues. In addition, there is the danger that a constant diet of fires could prove somewhat repetitive for the viewers. One of the biggest non-fire shouts was the train crash in series three which was based on the Clapham Junction, Moorgate, Kilburn and Leyton train crashes.

'I think the train crash was my most memorable shout,' says Gerry Mill. 'It was particularly difficult because we had to set it up from scratch. If you do anything with railways, British Rail don't always want to play ball and we had the added problem of doing a rail smash, which obviously British Rail didn't want us to. So we found a private railway, the Nene Valley, out at Peterborough and used a couple of their stock engines. We had to

buy some old carriages from a place in Leicester and these then had to be transported by road. They each weighed about 35 tons.

'We worked out how we wanted it. The carriages were turned on their sides and placed a foot apart. Some had to be cut in half which created an interesting poser for Colin Monk, our designer, and John Carman, our construction manager, who had to decide the best spot to do the cutting. The construction crew used acetylene torches and hacksaws and it worked a treat. They ripped the coaches apart, smashed the windows and the props guys appeared with what looked like a ton of dressing, things like suitcases scattered along the line, clothes and teddy bears. It took four days just to get it prepared.

'It nearly took even longer because when we arrived up at Peterborough there were high winds and for shifting the carriages we had the biggest crane that had been used in England. But it could only go up to a certain height depending on the wind conditions. Since this was virtually gale force, it was pretty tricky.

'We got a lot of co-operation from the local Fire Brigade and the local ambulance people. They provided us with a dozen fire appliances and crews and their families and children came along to play victims, all dressed up in blood and bandages. We had real ambulance people there and real paramedics playing themselves. So we created a situation where we stuffed 24 people in one carriage and 50 down the line wandering around in shock and everybody who came over the tops of carriages and climbed down through the chaos, everybody who was being treated by a paramedic, was being treated by a proper paramedic. So it looked, apart from the buckets of blood we were throwing over people, just like the real thing.

'We had got picture stills from several train crashes and had studied the rescue techniques of the men who were on duty. During the shoot, I constantly referred to the Fire Brigade stills and also to a video tape filmed during Clapham and other train crashes. They were my guidelines.

'In all, our scenes took 5 days to set up just for something like eight minutes of film,' says Gerry Mill. 'I think the crash scene cost about £100,000 but I was extremely pleased with the result. As the film was being processed at the labs overnight, at about three or four o'clock in the morning, apparently a guy walked in, looked at our rushes and gasped, "My God! There's been another train disaster." That was a great compliment.

'I showed that episode to the Brigade Chief and he shook me by the hand and said it was so real it made him feel quite strange. He wanted to use it as a training film for young firefighters.

'That was a really cold night up in Peterborough and I remember another time we nearly all froze to death was when we did a crane shout. The storyline was that a man was trapped in the cab of his crane some 200ft up. To film the rescue, we had to be up another crane level with him and we also had a second camera on top of the crane that this guy was trapped in. We were up there for four hours and it was snowing. It was so cold that after a while the cameraman on top of the crane couldn't move. He couldn't get down – it took him ages to get his limbs moving again. The trouble with those big unfolding cranes is that you can't just pop down to the ground every few minutes. There's no point in coming all the way down again, unless of course you feel the call of nature. But that was a nasty shout – I got bronchitis after that.'

Director Gerry Mill briefs actor Stephen North, alias raw recruit Colin.

Gerry Mill is living proof that being a director is not all exotic locations and bikini-clad girls. He ended up in a wheelchair after falling through a wall while filming the exciting light aircraft crash which heralded the start of the fourth series in September 1991. The plane was to land on a city centre roof but because the building used was listed, the crew had to build a false roof on which to stage the crash. This had to be a sound structure since it had to support a lot of people and so it was strengthened with 40ft high scaffolding and covered with plaster brickwork. The top 2ft was real brick and soft mortar to enable the fuselage of the crashed plane to be easily inserted. Unfortunately at one point the wall gave way and Gerry Mill fell through it, badly injuring his leg. He was taken to hospital but the show went on.

Gerry's injury wasn't the only mishap on the plane crash episode. 'To see the action from the pilot's point of view,' says Gerry, 'we got hold of a model radio-controlled helicopter with something like a 6ft wing span and strapped a video camera to it. Then we switched to a cine camera and had the helicopter fly straight at two tall chimneys before swerving at the last minute. Because it was all on a radio-controlled frequency, the guy who owned the helicopter had a finder that checks out all the local wavebands to see

The collapsing trench – the most miserable shout in the history of London's Burning. *So far...*

if there's, say a taxi, in the area. He checked absolutely everything and we did a "take". Come the second "take", he checked it all again meticulously. Tuning in, he found a free waveband and decided to use it. Alas just after he'd finished checking, it was a water board van I think which drove into the area and said something. So this helicopter got up to about 50ft, then suddenly went out of control. It spun round and round and disappeared into the docks. The helicopter sank and the little camera went down with it. We put in a team of divers and they managed to pull out the camera. Luckily the film was OK and we got some wonderful shots. But I'm afraid the helicopter was written off.'

To film the actual crash scene, three light aircraft were needed. A hired plane was used for aerial shots and two others were recruited from an aeroplane graveyard and painted to match the first. One stayed on the ground and was used for scenes inside the aircraft. To create the illusion of the plane getting into difficulties with the pilot transmitting a Mayday message, the stationary cockpit was rocked back and forth by the crew – the oldest trick in the book but still one of the most effective. The third plane was cut into pieces with a chainsaw and angle grinders and hoisted on to the false roof. Then one piece was rammed into the parapet. The chicanery didn't end there. Even the moving 'blips' of light, seen when a plane crosses the radar screen, were made by a man lurking behind a photograph with a tiny lightbulb on the end of a long stick. But with the help of a real air traffic controller who acted as consultant on this episode, the result was a thoroughly convincing disaster scene.

One part that was genuine was the actors' involvement. They had to climb a 45ft ladder, race across the roof with stretchers and oxygen tanks, then carry the victims down to a waiting ambulance. It provided an excellent test of the skills they had acquired in training. Stephen North, who plays Colin, says: 'The best thing about it was that it was shot in one go instead of stopping and starting. That makes it easier for us – we feel as if we're doing it for real.'

If there was an award for the most miserable shoot on *London's Burning*, one despised by cast and crew alike, there would only be one possible winner – the collapsing trench on episode four of the third series. The story was set on a building site and for filming purposes, an acre of mud was rented at New Cross in South-East London. It had a building site behind (a branch of McDonald's was being constructed) and so the *London's Burning* acre looked like part of the building site. Then a huge hole was dug to contain Colin Monk's 60ft long, 8ft deep purpose-built designer trench.

Filming the trench episode was a highly complicated – and often uncomfortable – exercise.

The trench itself was one big special effect. The 'mud' was principally coloured porridge with a heavy helping of polystyrene added to obtain the effect of shingle and shale. It was banked up at the sides and the collapse was achieved with the help of planks of wood all on hinges. Hidden alongside the trench were the various camera positions, sunk underground. And just for good measure, an overhead crane simulated non-stop rain.

'It really was the grottiest location imaginable,' says director of photography Geoff Harrison. 'Because of the water everywhere, all the trucks were getting stuck. One camera had to be down in that mud for a day and a half. That camera position was dug out sideways from the trench to obtain shots at "collapse level". It was like a little hide with layers of wood, mud and corrugated iron and yet more mud on top. So from above, you couldn't see it was there. It was completely hidden.

'There was all this stuff collapsing around the camera crew and if one bit had gone wrong, they wouldn't have got out because they were under it all too. You can still drown in porridge and it doesn't even sound heroic!'

Director John Reardon concedes: 'It was unbearable. It was my decision to put rain over the whole thing so for three days, the cast and crew suffered non-stop. I think it was the most difficult shoot I've had to do – certainly the most uncomfortable.'

Going underground. Blue Watch rescue a man trapped beneath a tube train – and all because he dropped his filofax. It really would have been easier to buy a new one.

Another of John Reardon's episodes was the story in the fourth series where a man was crushed under a London Underground train. The original intention was for it to be a suicide attempt to reflect the number of 'jumpers' on the Underground system. However London Transport were not in favour of that idea and so the script was amended. Instead a yuppie-type, somewhat the worse for wear, was seen to drop his beloved filofax on to the line and, despite warnings from his friend, he insisted on clambering down to retrieve it. Unfortunately, he was still there when the next train arrived.

'We filmed it at Aldwych Station,' says John Reardon, 'on the little stretch of line from Holborn. It's closed anyway at weekends so we had it all to ourselves and London Transport kindly switched off the power on the tracks. On the track we placed a four-wheel trolley behind Colin Monk's replica of the front of a tube train. The cameraman and myself stood on the trolley and we photographed through the fake front. Meanwhile the crew pushed the trolley along to give the impression of the driver coming towards the man on the track.

'For the same episode, I also did a hotel fire. We were looking for a location around Earl's Court or King's Cross but in a previous series we had used an old hospital at Wandsworth. I remembered it and Colin Monk cleverly made it look like a hotel.

'It was a six-storey building and one of the problems on these shouts is that the flames get so high that the local residents keep phoning the Fire Brigade. Although the location manager posts leaflets to people living nearby, this fire could be seen for miles across London. You can't leaflet everyone. Nor can you stop people seeing the fire and ringing up the Fire Brigade. No matter how often Nobby phoned Brigade HQ to tell them we were filming *London's Burning*, they kept coming out. Every five minutes we'd hear the sirens. You see, the Fire Brigade are obliged to respond to every call – they don't have time to check. After all, it could be a matter of life or death. You wouldn't want to dial 999 and have to wait while they checked whether a television series was being filmed that night. In the meantime your house could be burning down. Before doing *London's Burning*, I spent four days at Dockhead and there were a lot of false alarms but they always go out. They're terrific. In London, they guarantee that they'll be with you within five minutes of any shout. I really am a great fan of the Fire Brigade.'

It was much the same when John Reardon filmed the huge ship explosion aboard the *Lord Amory* which was docked near the Isle of Dogs. Location manager Kevin Holden says: 'The explosion took place at 9 pm and it was a very loud bang. We had leafleted people nearby but within a couple of minutes, six fire appliances turned up along with a couple of police motorcycles and 15 local residents. I spent the next hour apologising to the residents.'

Fortunately, no boy stood on the burning deck when the ship went up in flames.

John Reardon adds: 'The *Lord Amory* belongs to the Sea Scouts. We wanted a larger ship but by using a wide-angle lens, we were able to make it look bigger than it really was. For the interior scenes, which were done on the "burn stage" at Jacob Street, we had something like 40ft of foam floating around. We had cast and cameras inside it with everyone in breathing apparatus. I talked afterwards to those who had been in the foam. They said they expected it to be white but it becomes black very soon. You can't see or hear a thing – it's a very strange feeling.'

Like his fellow director Gerry Mill, John Reardon confesses to a certain amount of unease about human torches. 'I did the scene at the DHSS office where a distraught man poured a can of petrol over his head and set fire to himself. Gabe Cronnelly was the stuntman and he was brilliant. But I'm always worried in case anyone does get hurt. It's up to the director to say "Cut" and any director will say, "Keep it going, don't cut the flame". It's a very dangerous line you're treading because somebody's life is at stake. I watch the crew and they go into these places in breathing apparatus to fight a fire on my

WARDROBE MISTRESS

There's no such thing as a day off for Wardrobe Mistress Lynnette Cummin. Often she'll be out doing her everyday shopping when she'll suddenly spot something that would be perfect for one of the characters in *London's Burning*.

'The day after Boxing Day, I was outside a shop when I found a perfect jumper for Kelly, George's wife. I ran inside and luckily it was in a sale. It was truly gruesome – it was white with a scottie dog on the front. But it was just right for Kelly who is awfully twee and getting worse. Her wedding dress was wonderful – she looked like one of those toilet roll covers!

'In my job, you have to think of the characters as real people. I get clothes from all sorts of places – markets, High Street shops, the Salvation Army. Second hand shops are ideal because you get used clothes there. You don't want everyone wearing new clothes – after all, people don't do that in real life. I reckon Colin is our naffest dresser – he's not a clothes man.

'Occasionally we do go shopping with the actors for clothes and sometimes the cast do refuse to wear what I've bought. Glen Murphy, who plays George, really didn't want to dress up as a baby in the charity pram race. He didn't want to wear a baby-gro. But the Director wanted him to so he didn't stand much of a chance. Because he was so reluctant, he looked grumpy when Kelly tried to put his baby hat back on him and that made it work well on screen.

'With the actual uniforms, we're helped a great deal by the Fire Brigade. We own the uniforms and Nobby advises us on who should wear what and also on any changes, anything new that's come in. Likewise the ambulance service are very helpful. Last year we used the new paramedics' uniforms before they were actually in service. The Thames Water Authority gave us invaluable assistance with the sewer shout because you can't get sewage boots from anywhere other than sewage workers. All these people are keen to help us because we don't like to misrepresent anything. We have to get it right.

'Of course I do use various tricks of the trade. For example when we had a pilot in an oil-spattered shirt for the plane crash episode, instead of real oil I used a mixture of treacle and charcoal powder. It doesn't smell very nice but it washes off easily.

'The firefighting actors wear the real Brigade clothing – it's civilians in fire scenes that are the problem for me. So I try not to dress civilians in synthetic fabrics because they melt rather than burn. And melting is more dangerous than burning because it burns on to the skin. Wool is the favourite fabric because it doesn't burn that fast and it doesn't flame. It smoulders.'

What happens to the clothes when they are finished with? 'We don't throw them away,' says Lynnette. 'They're usually burned in the end – they're used on a body somewhere...'

Unmentionable stains, like blood and oil, wash off easily.

behalf. That worries me sometimes. The crew go up 180ft cranes for me whereas I'm not going to go up there under any circumstances. The crew on *London's Burning* really are phenomenal. To be honest if we were working at the BBC, I don't think they'd allow it at all.'

The third regular director on *London's Burning* is Keith Washington who has worked on *Minder*, the TV detective film *Palmer* and *Casualty*. 'I once had to film a complicated ten-minute operation for an episode of *Casualty*,' he says, 'and the London Hospital have actually used it as a teaching aid. The big difference between *Casualty* and *London's Burning* is that on *Casualty* the director can physically be there whereas on *London's Burning*, because of all the breathing apparatus and so on for the fire scenes, you can't get in the middle and you can't always see exactly what's going on. I do know *Casualty* are impressed by *London's Burning* because they've been along to study how we do fires.'

Keith Washington certainly had something of a baptism of fire on *London's Burning*. After directing two episodes in the third series, he was put in charge of the biggest fire sequence the show had ever done – Anita Bronson's stunning double episode at the end of series four. The setting was to be a large warehouse and the centrepiece of the action would be the collapse of the warehouse wall, leaving Hallam and Bayleaf buried under the rubble.

The first thing to find was a location. Bearing in mind that for five nights there would be 60ft flames roaring into the air, this towering inferno could hardly be filmed in the middle of London. The fire would be seen all over the capital and the Brigade would be on constant call-out. After weeks of searching, Nobby Clark and location manager Kevin Holden were tipped off by Cambridgeshire Fire Brigade, who had co-operated with the series on the Peterborough train crash, about a disused chicory warehouse at St Ives that was due for demolition. Kevin Holden says: 'We came to an arrangement whereby we'd smash it up a bit and the following week the contractors would come along and knock it down completely.'

The logistics in planning such a huge blaze are enormous. It took over two months of preparation. To obtain such high flames, Tom Harris and his special effects team used liquid propane gas and it took 12 of them nine days to lay the 2,500ft of pipes around the buildings. The pipes were fed with the liquid propane from a 10-ton tanker. Tom Harris also made 180 flame bars for additional lighting.

'It was supposed to be a 20-pump fire,' says Keith Washington, 'but we had 11 fire appliances which we tried to make look like 20. We also had four ambulances, a turntable ladder, 7,000ft of hose and 65 Cambridgeshire and London firefighters who were all off-duty volunteers and who appeared in vision as well as providing safety cover. Some were used to extinguish any fire no longer being filmed. Obviously if you've got nearly 100 firemen fighting a fire, you can't teach a load of extras how to hold a hose. You have to use real firefighters. And they do get paid...

'There was one other consideration. There were houses on one side of the site in front of the warehouse but the other three sides all bordered on fenland. Since the setting was supposed to be London, I had to be careful not to shoot any fenland. Of course we had a few teething troubles. At the height of the fire, we were pumping 2,500 gallons of water per minute but because of a hosepipe ban in the area, we had to use a nearby lake as our supply.'

Producer Paul Knight says: 'We later received a letter of complaint about using the lake but we wrote back pointing out that we had re-stocked the lake and had in fact left it healthier than it was.'

But the water supply was no more than a minor irritation compared to the wall that refused to fall. 'The wall was a nightmare,' says Keith, still almost visibly shuddering at the recollection. 'I wanted the wall to collapse and break the back of two lorries. There was a lot of brick in that wall and once it's come down, that's it. You've got to get it. It was the very first shot we did because we had to bring the wall down to make the area safe. We were filming on virtually the longest day of the year. It went dark at 9.40 pm

The big warehouse fire was London's Burning's *most ambitious – and potentially dangerous – shout to date.*

and dawn came up at 4.10 in the morning. I only had six and a half hours to get it so I was under a lot of pressure.

'We had six cameras trained on the wall and the special effects guys were using explosives and hydraulic rams to get the wall to collapse correctly because I wanted it to come down to reveal a raging inferno behind. The wall was something like 70ft high and 2ft thick and the guys had weakened it beforehand so that it would topple more readily. They had also cut down both sides so that it was separate from the building.

'The big moment came. I was totally in the hands of the special effects boys. What I do in those situations is stand as far away as possible and let them get on with it. My main responsibility was to shout "Cut!" Anyway the wall exploded but didn't come down. It bowed out about 18 inches and went back in. There wasn't quite enough juice.

From 23 floors up, Sicknote abseils down the side of London Weekend's studio building to save a window cleaner. But by the time he got there, actor Riachard Walsh had been replaced by a stunt double.

'I gave it a minute and then shouted, "Cut!" I thought as soon as I shout, "Cut!", it will just fall down and we won't have it on camera and we'll be really stuck. It was going to take 12 hours to re-set the charges so we eventually did it the following night.'

On such flat countryside, the fire was a tourist attraction for miles around. Lanes leading to the site were packed with cars and sightseers as hundreds of people abandoned their homes to witness the wonderful world of television at 3.00. in the morning. The police had to cone off some lanes to stop people getting too close. But, as Nobby Clark is only too aware, it could all have ended in a disaster of epic proportions.

'Without doubt, the situation that arose at St Ives was the most dangerous in the history of *London's Burning*. Even with my experience, it was frightening. It was all down to the 10-ton tanker of liquid propane which we were using for the fire effects. One of the requirements for using that amount of liquid propane gas is that the tanker must always have an immediate exit so that in an emergency it can be disconnected and driven away. So there was no way the tanker could be blocked off. There is also a maximum length of hose that can be used to connect the tanker to the set so I couldn't have the tanker too far away.

'Liquid propane is safe unless it's near fire. I had got the tanker as far away from the blaze as possible but with 60ft flames coming out of the top of a 70ft high building, it was no easy matter. To protect the tanker from the heat, I had set up hoselines with safety crews on the jets so that the whole of the tanker could be encompassed in one fog of water. This also counteracted the threat of burning debris landing on the tanker because although it was a special effect, there was still some debris in the air. In addition I put three other high-pressure, large diameter jets into the air to create a curtain of water spray between the tanker and the fire. It was worrying. All the time while I was trying to get this fire started, at the back of my mind was this potential danger.

'Everything seemed fine until the wind suddenly changed direction and burning debris started blowing towards the propane tanker. The wind got even stronger and I saw debris falling too close to the tanker. That was when I called a halt to filming. It was far too dangerous to carry on and I couldn't guarantee everyone's safety. We just had to stop and wait for the weather conditions to improve.

'If that tanker had exploded, it could have created a thing called a B.L.E.V.E., a boiling liquid expanding vapour explosion. And that would have blown a hole in St Ives.' Amazingly throughout such a complex exercise, the only injury was a nose bleed.

A further footnote to the warehouse shout was that after seeing the episode, a man from the St Ives area wrote to *London's Burning* offering to let them demolish his factory. He said it was coming down soon anyway and he would be delighted if they would come and blow it up.

Keith Washington was particularly pleased with the way in which the anxious wives' and girlfriends' scenes dovetailed in perfectly with the fire. 'The domestics were inter related with the shout and that was difficult because since the actresses weren't on location, they weren't aware of the size of the fire. The intensity of their emotions had to match the scale of the shout. Thanks to all concerned, they did and it worked well.'

Keith Washington's directing debut on *London's Burning* had been in episode five of the third series. The major shout there was to a window cleaner trapped in his cradle high up the side of an office block until Sicknote abseiled down to the rescue.

'We practised the abseiling over the rooves at the Jacob Street studios with genuine firefighters to see how they did it technically. We did the real thing at Kent House, home of London Weekend Television on the south bank of the Thames. Wind was a big problem because the top of Kent House is 23 floors up. The insurance people were

Director Keith Washington lines up a shot.

57

NOBBY CLARK

Nobby Clark, the Fire Brigade liaison officer on *London's Burning*, knows only too well what it's like to be at the sharp end of a major disaster. He has been with the Brigade for 24 years and until recently was the uniformed station officer in the press office at the London Fire Brigade headquarters at Lambeth. 'Part of my responsibilities was to assist film and television in Fire Brigade matters – to be a spokesperson for the Brigade at an incident and to pass it on to the media, especially for the news.' He could be called away from advising *London's Burning* at any moment. The crew remember him being urgently summoned from a production meeting to attend a major shout. The next time they saw him was on the news, face covered in smoke and sweat, outside the scene of the King's Cross Underground fire.

He was also at Clapham Junction. 'What I remember most from that disaster was not the noise or the carnage but the birds singing in the trees and the silence. It was absolutely silent when I arrived.'

London's Burning is by no means Nobby's first involvement with a television series. 'A couple of years earlier, I had started work on *The Bill*. In fact, I still help out on fire scenes in *The Bill*. I've also worked on *Eastenders*, *Big Deal*, *Boon* and *Casualty*, usually script advising about firefighting scenes, so by the time I came to do *London's Burning* I had some insight as to how the television industry worked and what its requirements were.

'It was a very brave decision of the then Deputy Chief Officer of the London Fire Brigade, Gerry Clarkson, to give the agreement for *London's Burning* and I think he took a lot of flak from other fire chiefs who wanted LWT to come up with a boring two-hour PR film which nobody would have watched. At the start, it's fair to say that the majority of firefighters were anti but I think they've warmed to the show. They can see the value in it, that we can perhaps insert a fire safety message. We received a letter from the Chief Officer of the Merseyside Brigade congratulating us on the big warehouse fire. We've worked with the Kent Fire Brigade, Cambridgeshire, Surrey, Hampshire and of course London. They're all willing to help. They can see that the public information on *London's Burning* makes it worthwhile assisting.

'Also as a result of *London's Burning*, there is now no woman in Britain who doesn't know that it's possible to be in the fire service. When we started in 1986, there were only something like half a dozen women in the London Fire Brigade. Now there are over 50. But the reaction of the men in Jack Rosenthal's original film, that they didn't want a woman, was as it was then. Let's face it, if there's a fire in your house, it doesn't matter whether it's a man or a woman who kicks your door down to get you out of bed.

'The characters are totally realistic. If the majority of firefighters were truthful about it, they could put names to Colin, Sicknote and so on. These people exist. The Watch can be very rich in its language and very expressive towards one another but there's an easy way of stopping it all – and that's when the bells go down. Then they suddenly become the highest professionals.'

For someone with the surname Clark, Nobby is not the most original nickname in the world. But he has had plenty of experience of more inventive monikers. 'As an instructor teaching recruits, I had this guy whose name was Alan Toomey. I trained him for four months and had to deliver him to his station. I got there, drove into the yard and as soon as I opened the door, one of the Watch asked, "Have you got Sockit on board?"
I said, "Sockit?"
He said, "Yea, Sockit Toomey!"
And that's still his nickname.'

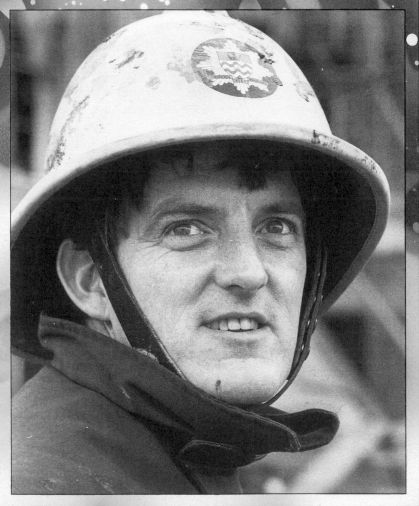

hanging around all the time, telling us that if the wind got above so many knots, they wouldn't let us do it.

'On screen, you actually saw Richard go over the edge of Kent House. What we did was build a false roof on top of Kent House so that I could take a shot of him disappearing over the edge and you could see the whole of London below. In truth, Richard, who was on a harness, had about 10ft to fall on to nice soft mattresses. I don't think any actor would have gone right over the side of Kent House – it is rather a long way down.'

Happily not every day's filming on *London's Burning* involves putting out fierce fires, scaling tower blocks or wading through damp, murky sewers. Much of the show's appeal lies in its humour and sometimes what goes on behind the scenes is even funnier than what appears on screen. Geoff Harrison remembers having particular problems with our feathered friends.

'We did an episode in which young Colin resuscitated an apparently dead budgie with his breathing mask and it flew to freedom out of the window. It was actually based on a true story. So we got this stuffed budgie and used a blast of air to propel it out of the window. Unfortunately we couldn't get enough air pressure to make it look as if it was flying without making the bird disintegrate. We ended up with 18 bits of budgie flying out of the window. We shot it in slow motion, wide angle, everything but no matter what we tried, the end result looked like a rock going through the air with a few feathers stuck on the end of it. And lumps of polystyrene budgie were flying in every direction.

'We tried it four times in all. We even attempted to make the budgie fly by propelling it with elastic bands. But we just could not get a shot of this budgie appearing to fly. Finally we had to cheat and settle for a shot of people on the ground looking up to the sky. We may be able to create spectacular fires and motorway pile-ups but we met our match with a polystyrene budgie!'

On another occasion, the crew stuck to the script a little too closely – and proceeded to lose a fire appliance. 'We were filming in Kent,' says Nobby Clark, 'on a story in which the Blackwall appliance, helping out the local Brigade, got lost on the way to a shout. Unfortunately while filming it, one of our engines really did go missing for a few hours.

One fire appliance that didn't get away...

'The crew had been filming in two different locations. We had taken two appliances to act as one. They were dressed to look similar so we could double one for the other just by changing the numbers on the side. One had a camera rig put on it and we thought it was coming back to base. We were patiently waiting at the location base but it didn't arrive. There was no sign of it. The camera department thought we were going to it so they had gone off. Thus in the depths of Kent we started searching for this fire engine. Fortunately the Kent Brigade eventually found it for us – it was just wandering around the lanes.'

There really is never a dull moment filming *London's Burning*. And the show's enormous popularity can have its drawbacks. Director Gerry Mill says: 'At first, people saw us out filming and thought we were doing a documentary. Now we get crowds of sightseers. Wherever we are, the location managers always put leaflets through letter-boxes saying that we're filming in the area. The trouble is the show is so popular that now when they get the letter, people tell their friends and they all turn up. Only recently we had 100 schoolgirls rocking the location dining bus one lunchtime because they saw Glen Murphy inside.

'We can't always film in a busy area. For instance we can't do fog scenes near a main road in case the smoke guns which produce the fog blow the wrong way and we could end up causing a real accident. Also I find that when drivers see filming lights, they are so concerned with finding out what's going on that they don't pay attention to the road.

'Filming *London's Burning* has certainly brought home to me the grim realities of fire. When I watch the news and hear that four children have burned in a fire, it used to be awful but now it's absolutely horrendous. You relive that which you have set up dramatically. You know what they've gone through.

'My house is full of smoke alarms now whereas before doing *London's Burning*, I would never have dreamed of buying one.'

Director Gerry Mill prepares to go over the top.

After his initial stage debut in a nativity play at school in Deal, Rupert Baker's acting career could only go in one direction – up.

'I was seven or eight at the time and I played a shepherd. I had a mate called Ross who wore blue-framed National Health Service glasses like the Milky Bar Kid and had a sticking plaster over one eye. He was a shepherd too. We had snooker cues as crooks and in the course of the play, I nearly put his good eye out with my cue. Who needed a mate like me!'

Strictly speaking, the school nativity was not Rupert's first attempt to break into showbusiness. 'I gave a conjuring show in my mum's living room when I was five. I pulled all these knotted handkerchiefs out of a marine's hat (we couldn't find a top hat). That was the end of my career as a magician – I decided to leave the field to Paul Daniels.'

School plays enabled Rupert to make his mark. 'I was dyslexic so a lot of academic work was lost on me. I used to play the fool to get out of tricky situations. The reading I was able to crack and catch up with but I never caught up with the maths. I've never passed a maths exam in my life.

'The first film I ever saw was Norman Wisdom's *The Early Bird* which I was taken to by my father. He also took me round Deal Fire Station because he was a doctor and worked at the hospital and so had links with the local Brigade. I remember being shown the pole they all slid down. Little did I know I would be doing the same many years later.'

Norman Wisdom became something of a role model for young Rupert. 'For me who couldn't read or write and had terrible co-ordination, he was my ideal. He mucked everything up. I wanted to be Norman Wisdom. It was he more than anybody that got me interested in acting.'

Rupert's interest in the stage grew from going to the cinema to see films such as *Becket* (with Peter O'Toole and Richard Burton), *Lawrence of Arabia* (again with O'Toole) and *A Man For All Seasons* starring Paul Scofield. 'One of my teachers told me I'd never be an actor because of my dyslexia and

other people warned that acting didn't pay. But the more I was told I couldn't do it, the more I wanted to. I really developed a taste for it. I thought, "Well, somebody's doing it."'

On leaving school, Rupert studied graphic design and spent three years at the Webber Douglas Academy studying theatre. 'To feed myself, because I was out of work for 16 months, I formed a two-man cabaret act, The Savoy Boys, a sort of budget version of Manhattan Transfer. I was in a Catch-22 situation where I couldn't get an Equity card unless I had a job and I couldn't get a job unless I had a Card. So one way to get my ticket was through variety.'

The Savoy Boys played London's top hotels and when they got their ticket, they promptly disbanded. Rupert recalls one particularly excruciating booking at a hotel near Maidstone. 'We had lied to get it, saying that we could do a Cockney knees-up, whereas in our dinner jackets we were more lounge crooners. We were completely unsuitable for a Cockney knees-up – it was like sending Noel Coward down to Millwall. Anyway we died a death because we had no repertoire and they turned the juke boxes on – the ultimate ignominy.'

One of Rupert's first major roles was as pot-smoking art director Scott Golding in Les Blair's acclaimed film about an advertising agency *Honest, Decent and True*. Golding was an ardent fan of *The Prisoner* and Les Blair made Rupert join the Six of One Club, the Prisoner appreciation society. And when Les Blair came to direct the original film of *London's Burning*, he remembered Rupert and eventually cast him as Malcolm.

'When I went to see Les Blair for the audition, I thought it was for some sort of training film for the Brigade. When I learned that Jack Rosenthal had written it, I was gobsmacked. It was a real shot in the arm for my career because prior to that I had even been thinking about joining the Army.'

Malcolm is a decent cove, from a higher social order than the rest of the men at Blackwall. Behind his suave ladies' man image, there lurks a tender heart – remember his inconsolable grief at the death of pretty Asian girl Samina in the sweatshop fire. The recipient of a bravery award for the trench shout, Malcolm has recently been wooing his law student lodger Helen.

'Malcolm is the odd one out on the Watch,' says Rupert. 'He gets his leg pulled by the others because he is a public school misfit. In that respect alone he is like me because to overcome my dyslexia, I was sent to public school – Dover College. When the Jack Rosenthal film came out, nobody believed that there were people like Malcolm in the Fire Brigade. But there are. One of the writers found a press cutting about a baronet who drove a Morgan and there was also an ex-BBC radio announcer in the Brigade who spoke immaculately.'

Rupert, who has also appeared in *The Vikings, Cabaret* (where he played a Nazi) and the controversial Falklands War drama *Tumbledown*, has literally warmed to *London's Burning*. 'The sweatshop scene was extremely hot,' he says. 'I had to go in without breathing apparatus and they had to shut the doors. Flames were going up all around me then the stairs started to catch. I said, "Can we get out soon because the stairs are going?" If you go past a certain point, you've lost it and the whole lot will go because if you burn anything long enough, it will catch fire even if you fire-proof it.

'With breathing apparatus, you have to pace your breathing or you would use up your tanks. You have to keep breathing steadily – not gasping. They're awkward things to get into. You want to do it just right but at first you get tied in terrible knots and end up looking really silly.

'I remember the first sewer shout we did, at Beckton Sewage Works. You can imagine having location breakfast at 7.30 in the morning next to the smell of sewage. They used a dry shaft and built an underground river and a tank. We wore dry suits but in fact they were anything but. I got into this tank and within 30 seconds water was trickling in over my toes and then steadily working its way up my leg. Over the next hour and a half, I turned steadily blue and got colder and colder. Luckily when we went back in after a break, Glen Murphy got the dodgy suit. It was serious suffering for our art.

'But every actor loves getting stuck in to the shouts – it makes you forget you've got flat feet in real life. It's Steve McQueen time, a good lark. If you're cold, everybody gives you brandy and blankets afterwards and that's a good arrangement.'

Rupert is 31, single and lives in West London. His great passion is his Harley-Davidson motorcycle and he belongs to the Gravesend Eagles club. 'When I rode it in to *London's Burning* once and parked on location, the cast sneaked out and poured oil underneath the bike. Then they pointed out, "There's oil – your bike's got a leak." I thought, "Damn!" Then I cottoned on.

'I've played some good jokes too, though. The best was when Glen Murphy and I wrote Sean Blowers out of the second series, instead of Vaseline. Because Paul Knight didn't want anyone to get hold of what happened to Vaseline, that section of script was held back. So we wrote a dummy section in which Sean's character Hallam was killed off. We got everyone in on it, the office duplicated it and it was officially handed out.

'We kept it going for a bit and then Sean went for an audition for something else. So we thought we'd better ring his agent who rang ahead to tell Sean it was a wind-up.'

Young East End boxer Glen Murphy was in the middle of a training session when talent scouts from the nearby Half Moon Theatre came in looking for likely lads for a forthcoming production.

Glen recalls: 'They wanted a couple of boxers for the opening night of their play, *Johnny Boxer*, to add a bit of authenticity in the background. The other guy who was chosen had a fight come up so in the end it was just me, sparring on stage with the lead actor.

'Apart from Christmas plays at school, that was the first acting I'd ever done. But I knew a few of the people at the Half Moon – one of the actresses worked as a barmaid in my dad's pub – and afterwards they said there was a job there if I was interested. So I joined the Half Moon as an Assistant Stage Manager for a year. And that's how I first got into acting.'

Glen was raised in Canning Town, very much part of a boxing background. 'My dad Terry was a British champion, my uncle Joe Lucy won a Lonsdale Belt and my uncle Eddie Wright once fought Randolph Turpin.

'My dad knew the Krays through boxing. They used to send me Christmas presents when I was little. One year Ronnie gave me some fairy stories.

'My first fight was when I was nine and I used to train every night. I became British Schoolboy Champion and went on to fight for England as an amateur. I sparred with people like John H. Stracey and Maurice Hope. In all I had 80 bouts as an amateur yet actually I was a better footballer than a boxer. As a striker, I played for Chelsea as a schoolboy in the same team as Ray Wilkins and then I became an apprentice professional with Charlton.'

After his job at the Half Moon, Glen, who had married his childhood sweetheart Linda at 16, went back to boxing and briefly turned professional, winning both of his fights. Then a second accidental meeting, this time with boxer turned film entrepreneur George Walker, changed Glen's career plans for good.

'George came up to me at a family wedding and said, "You've got a good face, you want to forget about boxing." And he introduced me to a chap who ran a film company. I did a few odd jobs and then I was offered two days' work on the film *Victor/Victoria*.

'I started weighing it all up. I was getting £300 a fight as a boxer, of which I took home about £120, but on *Victor/Victoria* I would be getting £200 a

day, so that's £400 for the two days, just pretending to be a boxer. Also I got to meet people like Blake Edwards and James Garner and there was no danger of me being hurt. I didn't need much persuading and I although I had a wife, two kids and a mortgage, I decided to give acting a go.

'I got my first theatre contract at the same time as I was running a famous pub called the Bridge House in Canning Town. It was a great place for music. We had Mick Jagger in there and we started off the likes of Depeche Mode and Paul Young.'

But all that took a back seat to acting, and Glen polished his technique by watching Marlon Brando in *On The Waterfront* at every available opportunity.

Glen says: 'I started at the time of films like *Raging Bull* and *Rocky* so there was suddenly a lot of call for boxers on television. And I had one big advantage over the rest – I was the real McCoy.'

At first, Glen mainly played boxers, as in *Seconds Out* with Robert Lindsay and *Shine On Harvey Moon* where he was Alfie, Linda Robson's fiance. 'I was a bit scared doing Harvey Moon because I was still green but Linda Robson was great. She showed me the ropes.'

Further series followed including *The Other 'Arf*, *Murphy's Mob* and *Prospects* until Glen landed the part of ex-boxer George in *London's Burning*. 'I used to box with Terry Marsh who was also a fireman and I used him as my role model for George. Terry helped me a lot, particularly with the emotional side of how firemen react to fires and tragedies.'

There is also a lot of Glen in George. 'Obviously since our backgrounds are the same, I've added something of myself to the part. I didn't want to make George the typical punch-drunk boxer with lots of sniffing – I didn't want to make him a caricature. We've managed to keep George fresh by showing his sensitive side because although he is a very macho character, he's got a wife Kelly and a baby on the way. George could prove himself in a crowd if he had to but he doesn't want to. And that goes for me too.'

Thirty-five-year-old Glen, who has four children – Glastra, 19, Glen Junior, 16, Natalia, 6, and Emilio, 3 – has never regretted switching from boxing to acting. 'Being in a hit series like *London's Burning* has opened so many doors for me. For a start, it's enabled me to play on most of the London football grounds. As a West Ham fan since the age of three, it was like a dream come true when I scored at Upton Park in a testimonial game.

'And earlier this year, me and my cousin Tom Lucy, who's a stunt man and has doubled for me on *London's Burning*, played at Wembley in a celebrity match before the ZDS Cup Final. In front of a crowd of 70,000, we walked into the centre circle and hugged each other. We just couldn't believe this was happening to two lads from Canning Town.'

STATION OFFICER NICK GEORGIADIS

When no-nonsense Nick Georgiadis succeeded avuncular Sidney Tate as Station Officer at Blackwall, it sent shock waves rippling through Blue Watch. It was like Attila the Hun taking over from Russell Grant.

On his powerful motor-bike, Greek Cypriot Nick was clearly a man of action and he started by reading the riot act to Hallam, who, having been rejected for promotion himself, clearly disapproved of his new boss. Nick was determined to stamp his authority on the Watch, no matter how unpopular it made him. Yet gradually a more mellow side appeared although he has so far failed to match the dancing connotations of his none too original nickname Zorba. He proceeded to win everyone's respect through his athleticism and professionalism and was even justified in laying out a drunken Kevin during a family party at Uncle Demetri's restaurant. Indeed Nick began to attract viewers' sympathy as he struggled to resist mounting family pressure for him to marry his cousin Ariadne.

Born in Cyprus, Andrew Kazamia came to live in South London when he was four. He left school at 16 and worked as a milkman near to where *London's Burning* is now filmed. 'I know all the locations. I had a milk round in the area but gave it up because it was tedious and many people couldn't pay their bills.' He also got a job as a vending machine operator and worked in the stables of a quarantine station, cleaning out endless piles of muck.

He also went to sea as an entertainments officer. 'I was 25 and on one liner I was bingo-caller to 1,200 retired women on a world cruise.'

Now 36, Andrew, who has appeared in *Widows*, *The Family* and *Inspector Morse*, is married with two sons, five-year-old Alexandro and three-year-old Constantine. He describes himself as 'a true family man.'

The physical demands of *London's Burning* have presented few problems for Andrew. He doesn't mind climbing ladders but confesses that he's not always too comfortable when he's at the top. 'The worst moment is when you hook yourself on top of a ladder and let go. You can't fall off because you are hooked on, but try telling your brain that!'

Shortly after landing the part, he sampled first-hand experience of the work of the Fire Brigade. 'I was at a barbecue when suddenly one of the guests' cars caught fire and went up in smoke. Happily, the Brigade came swiftly and dealt with the blaze very efficiently. They are a brave bunch and I wouldn't like their job. They live on the edge of life.'

Nick's dark Mediterranean looks have already made him a favourite with women viewers. Andrew laughs it all off. 'I would be just as thrilled to get letters from grans and grandads as I would from young women.'

'I'd have run through a burning building with no clothes on just to have got the part in *London's Burning*.' This unlikely claim is made by Sean Blowers, alias Blackwall's dour Sub-Officer Hallam.

'At the time I was in the West End doing the Elvis play *Are You Lonesome Tonight?*' says Sean who is mercifully nothing like his screen character. 'One of my best friends is Jerome Flynn who I met at drama school and I'd heard him talking about how he had got a part in this new film *London's Burning*. He was playing a character called Rambo. I thought it sounded great. Anyway some time after he was chosen, I got an interview too. It was fantastic to be picked – we were kicking each other under the table.'

Sean admits that he fell into acting. 'I was at a loss as to what to do with my life. I went to an all boys' school, St. Joseph's College at Ipswich, which was very sport-minded. There were no openings for acting. My first introduction to drama was for "O" Level when, in a class full of boys, I had to read Juliet in *Romeo and Juliet*. I suffered for that. But the teacher took us to see Zeffirelli's *Romeo and Juliet* and that, although I didn't realise it at the time, had a fairly profound effect on me. Until then, I had thought that acting was all rubbish but that was so beautiful, I realised there was more to it. And Olivia Hussey was absolutely stunning.'

But Sean was still in limbo when he left school. He considered doing business studies or joining the Marines but in the end settled for touring America with a friend. 'I was out there for six months and I really enjoyed it. I did all sorts of odd jobs including carpet laying and swimming pool maintenance (apparently Clint Eastwood used to do swimming pool maintenance). That got my natural wandering out of my system and then I came back to Britain to do something properly.

'I thought it would be a good idea to work in a theatre. So I became a stage-hand at the Wolsey Theatre, Ipswich. I started off sweeping up and then driving the van, gradually getting more involved.

My first stage role was as a six-foot yellow chicken!'

After attending the Central School of Speech and Drama for a more formal training, Sean appeared in a number of television series including *Me and My Girl*, *Hot Metal*, *The Bill* and *Minder*. 'I was also in *Crossroads* during the show's final year. I played Tony, the overweight Botswana beef salesman from Walthamstow – that was my character description. Tony nearly drowned in the Motel pool and exited on a stretcher. I did about eight episodes in all. There was a time when nobody would admit to having been in *Crossroads* but I'm actually quite proud of it. The turnaround on the show was frightening. There was so little time. I've got the utmost respect for soap opera actors.'

Another of Sean's roles caught up with him when he went to the theatre one night. 'This kid came up to me. I thought he had recognised me from *London's Burning* because I had been doing that for two years by then but instead he said: "You were in *Dr. Who*, you played a rebel." And he reeled off the episode title, the lot. I was staggered – I was only in one episode and then only for the first 30 seconds!'

As second-in-command at Blackwall, Hallam was bitter about being overlooked for the station officer's job when Tate left. He made no attempt to disguise his resentment to Tate's successor, Nick Georgiadis. The atmosphere between them was decidedly frosty. Being the 'guv' would have given Hallam the chance to exercise his authority – something he is incapable of doing at home when confronted with his perpetually nagging wife Sandra, a pit-bull terrier in a pinny. First he had to put up with his elderly father-in-law as a lodger until the old man eloped with a resident from the local old people's home. Then, after being the victim of a practical joke, he was accused by Sandra of having an affair and exiled to the spare room. And finally there was the furore over Sandra's new kitchen. Blue Watch agreed to fit it but a mix-up over the size of the window-frame left a gaping hole in the wall for what seemed like an eternity. Sandra was not amused.

'Basically Hallam is boring,' admits Sean. 'He is very straight and career-orientated. He's good enough to get on but it's a slow process. He doesn't shine but he's solid and reliable. Yet he becomes a sympathetic character because of Sandra. I get a lot of reaction from the public who sympathise with me about Sandra. Men come up to me and say, "Yea, I get all that too. My wife's driving me mad about a new kitchen, just the same. I know what you're going through." But I'd hate to think I was much like Hallam. He worries me.'

Hallam certainly had plenty on his mind after being trapped under the collapsed wall in the big warehouse fire. He refused to accept counselling, preferring to bottle up his feelings before breaking down uncontrollably when told by Nick that he was not fit to return to duty.

'It was a very powerful end to the fourth series,' says Sean. 'The beauty of it was that people were so used to seeing Hallam coping with everything, never being thrown, and then he crumbled. And crying on Sandra's shoulder humanised her too.

'The scenes were very realistic but not nearly as horrific as what happens in real life. Our job was to set the scene in a dramatic way, to put over the idea of how terrible fire can be – and the idea of being in any sort of fire fills me with dread. I simply can't imagine what goes through the mind of someone trapped who is absolutely convinced there's no escape.'

Like everyone else on *London's Burning*, Sean has few fond memories of the trench shout. 'I think on a scale of one to ten, that was probably a nine point five. Every now and then we do get a shout which is miserable and that was one of the most miserable you could ever get. We did it in February and it was very cold. There was a crane from above with water simulating rain so whichever way you looked, you were wet. The real Brigade would have been in and out but on *London's Burning* we were in and in – for three days. All the time I was thinking, "Please let this be the last 'take'."

'There are similarities between firefighters and acting on TV – you do have a lot of time on your hands and you do tend to spar off each other. In the public eye, the Fire Brigade can do no wrong – they're everyone's favourite heroes like lifeboatmen. So the reaction I get in the street is always good, unlike some guys who appear in *The Bill* who may go into a pub and find someone wanting to take a pop at them simply because they're playing a copper. And real firefighters are always coming up to us and saying, "We've got a Colin, we've got a Sicknote." That's why *London's Burning* is a winner.'

Sean, 31, lives in Twickenham with wife Shirley and children Kimberley, eight, and Rory, five. Along with co-star Rupert Baker, he is a Harley-Davidson freak.

'I've been mad about bikes for three years. I thought, "I'm in a reasonably steady job, I've got a super wife, two lovely children, the house, the car – I'm not going to go out chasing other women so maybe I'll get a bike." My bike is my mistress. Bikes are a great drug – I'd recommend them to anybody.

'What I'd really like to do one day is go round the world on a Harley-Davidson. It's a bit more daring than Hallam. He'd settle for London to Brighton in a Ford Sierra...'

Stuart MacKenzie is known as Recall because of his totally incredible photographic memory. Show him the page of a book and he will be able to recite it word for word after the merest glance. But actor Ben Onwukwe confesses: 'My own memory is appalling. Recall and I are far apart. I am infamous in my family for not remembering birthdays and anniversaries.

'It's so bad that I'm often tempted by those newspaper advertisements offering, "Improve Your Memory". I haven't written off yet but I think there will come a time when I'll have to, particularly if I start being unable to memorise scripts.'

Ben is very fond of Recall. 'He's a decent, ordinary, hard-working guy. But he and his wife Laura have this situation at home where their young son Jamie has cystic fibrosis. This drives Recall to be even more conscientious in his responsibilities to the public at large and to his son. In the mess, he tends to be the one who is ready to have a laugh which in a way hides his inner torment about having a son with a crippling disease.

'The idea for the cystic fibrosis storyline in the fourth series originated at a production meeting for *London's Burning*. People were talking about various rare diseases and quite a few there knew someone who suffered from cystic fibrosis. I met people from cystic fibrosis organisations to find out how the parents cope in such situations. And coping's the word because you never know when your child's going to have an attack.'

In *London's Burning*, it was Bayleaf who found out about Jamie and sounded out the Watch about organising a pram race to raise enough money to send the boy to Disneyworld. The race was a great success with Blackwall firefighters and nurses from Great Ormond Street Children's Hospital all in fancy dress pushing prams and trolleys through the streets of South-East London. They raised over £1,000.

Not for the first time, the cast of *London's Burning* helped out for real in a charitable cause. While filming the pram race, they themselves collected over £500 for cystic fibrosis.

Ben says: 'Without overdoing it as an issue, it was nice to be able to use the programme to draw people's attention to something like cystic fibrosis.

'Then in the next episode I was trapped beneath a beam with my foot on fire in the huge warehouse blaze. That was a bit uncomfortable but of course the truth is I was doing it all inside a studio where a cup of tea is only five seconds away.'

Thirty-four-year-old Ben lives in North London with his schoolteacher wife Patrice and children Maya, aged 5 and Leo, 2. He first developed an interest in acting at school.

'I went to a boarding school near Ipswich called Woolverstone Hall. It's not there anymore but it was set up to provide a grammar school situation for London schoolboys. I wasn't a particularly good pupil academically but I did seem to shine in school productions, so much so that the English master took me to one side and said, "Have you considered doing this for a career?"

'It had never entered my head. For one thing, we never had a television set in the house – my mother had a strange obsession with what television does to the mind. It meant I felt a bit left out in some school conversations. When you go back to boarding school after the holidays, there are the usual pleasantries like "What did you get up to?" and then talk turns to what's been on television. The other kids were going on about *The Avengers* and *The Saint* but of course I missed out. Mind you, I'm a bit of a couch potato now – I'm making up for lost time.'

Following 'A' Levels, Ben toured France and Italy before coming home to do a degree in performing arts at Middlesex Polytechnic. 'I think I did the course because I had this desire to prove that I was academic. I came from a family to whom education was very important. But the course wasn't really a grounding for an actor.

'Once I graduated from there, the struggle began. I was unemployed for nine months and then got a job as a drama tutor on a Youth Opportunities Scheme. My fellow graduates and I dreamed up this YOPS programme for unemployed kids who were interested in the performing arts and we managed to secure an arrangement with the Commonwealth Institute in Kensington.

I did that for a year but then I saw the futility of it. All it was doing was keeping kids off the streets. It was all about showing what we could do – I don't think it helped them much.

'I then seriously considered finding real acting work. My first acting job was at the Elephant Theatre in a one-act play called *Put Your Shoes On Lucy*. I played a psychiatrist.'

Ben finally got the much-coveted Equity Card in 1982 through the Black Theatre Co-Operative. His TV debut was in *The Bill* in which he played a sergeant visiting Sun Hill. He has also appeared in *Bergerac* ('I was a sports hero in the mould of Daley Thompson, being pursued by drug peddlars') and *Inspector Morse* as a pathologist. Immediately prior to joining *London's Burning*, he worked for BBC Radio Rep for 15 months.

'The training course on *London's Burning* certainly gave me an interesting insight into the lives of firefighters. Before that, I hadn't much idea about what they did. I enjoyed the course although I wasn't too keen on the high ladders.

'The hardest part of all was joining a hit show. It was a bit like your first day at school. I'd heard all about the cast's practical jokes and I was looking over my shoulder every day. Whenever I opened the door, I checked first that there wasn't a cup of water perched on top of it. Touch wood, they haven't managed to get me – yet.'

No matter how tough the going gets on London's Burning, Ross Boatman never complains. He just thinks back to the days when he had to get up at the crack of dawn to put goldfish into plastic bags!

'After leaving school, I spent a few years doing odd jobs,' says 26-year-old Ross. 'I did some labouring work and I also worked at Hampstead Fair for a year. One of my jobs was to put goldfish into plastic bags as prizes and it meant putting my hands into icy cold water at 7 o'clock in the morning. It was terrible.

'I much preferred working on the dodgems. I was a teddy boy at the time so it was perfect for me.'

Ross's showbusiness career began in the time-honoured tradition of doing impersonations at junior school. 'I did all the usual ones – people like Frank Spencer and Tommy Cooper. Everyone at school did impressions but when I did them, people laughed. It was a nice feeling because I was very shy as a kid and it got me noticed.

'I moved on to a London comprehensive school which had a good drama department. But I was still too shy to put myself forward and it wasn't until we started doing drama classes that were part of the

curriculum that the drama teacher noticed me. I played a comic down-and-out biker in a school play (his bike had blown to pieces so he had to use a push-along scooter) and the acting took off from there. I ended up doing all the school shows.

'I was a complete failure academically, though. The only things I excelled at were gambling, girlfriends and smoking – I learned how to get lucky in love and cards! I couldn't see the point of exams so I spent more time down at the local cafés playing pinball and chatting up girls. The result was I left school at 15 without any qualifications.'

But Ross hadn't lost his interest in acting and after his succession of odd jobs, he studied drama for a year at a Further Education College. He then spent the next couple of years touring Europe and working in London fringe theatre.

But then a chance phone call changed his life. 'The principal of RADA rang up to speak to a girlfriend of mine. I answered it and managed to talk my way into an audition.'

During his two years with RADA, he appeared in a dozen productions and, again through a lucky

encounter – this time on the London Underground – a hard-hitting anti-heroin TV advertisement.

Fresh from RADA, Ross began working with Simon Callow at the Theatre Clwyd in *Amadeus* and has gone on to appear in the Merchant/Ivory film *Maurice* and on television in such programmes as *All In Good Faith* and *The Storyteller*. But obviously it is the role of the troubled, often surly, but basically kind-hearted, Kevin in *London's Burning* that has been his biggest break to date.

'It's a great series to do,' says Ross. 'I remember for the big warehouse fire, they set the whole yard alight and Richard Walsh and I went in with a fully-charged hose which normally would have three, four or five real firefighters holding it because the pressure is so powerful. It was very slippery because there was three or four inches of mud and it was really hot. It felt like my face was swelling with the heat so it was adrenalin, heart-pumping stuff. It was tremendously exciting, probably the nearest I've got to real firefighting.'

Many years before he joined *London's Burning*, Stephen North had good reason to be grateful to the Fire Brigade as he became involved in a web of calamity that would not have disgraced his screen alter ego, the accident-prone Colin Parrish.

'I'd left school and was with the Pegasus Youth Theatre in Oxford,' recalls Stephen. 'A group of us were at a mate of mine's flat. Actually it was his parents' flat but they were away on holiday. I smoked at the time and as I put my cigarette out, the ashtray fell on to a cushion. I saw what happened and put some water on it. Anyway, we all went off to see a film but when we got back three hours later, black smoke was pouring out of the windows. The cigarette ash had caught fire and smouldered. Luckily the neighbours had called the Fire Brigade.

'Inside, all the walls were black and the chair was destroyed but fortunately the flat itself hadn't caught fire. We had to spend four hours cleaning off the walls and then we left my mate to it. I still see him occasionally and I don't think his mum and dad ever did find out!'

The role of Colin marks Stephen's television debut. Born in Dorking and raised in Wantage, Oxfordshire, he appeared in various school productions and spent two years with the Pegasus. He then attended the Guildford School of Acting where he played a teddy boy in the end-of-year show *Once A Catholic*. Little did he know that it would lead directly to his job on *London's Burning*.

'Although I was unaware of it at the time, Corinne Rodriguez, the casting director on *London's Burning*, saw me in *Once A Catholic*. I think I was spotted because the part was a bit similar to that of Colin, in that they are both typical teenagers, both coming on all strong but really they are not. Anyway I left college and did a tour and a year later Corinne rang me up. I didn't even have an agent. She said, "It's Corinne Rodriguez from *London's Burning*. We're interested in you for this part." I thought it was a wind-up.'

But Stephen went along and landed the part. Corinne Rodriguez remembers that the moment he walked into the room, she knew she had found her ideal Colin. Stephen is not sure whether to be flattered or not...

'As an actor, I was a bit like Colin as a fireman,' admits Stephen, 'keen and trained but a bit naive. I'd never done any TV at all – I hadn't a clue about the technical side of it. I was thrown straight in at the deep end. I think I spent the first six months wandering around bemused – all the terminology was completely foreign to me. I found it very

daunting, and also coming into a series that had been running for two years, where everyone knew everyone, the crew knew everyone, made me feel very much the new boy. I was full of insecurity and paranoia, hoping that I would be all right.

'The Fire Brigade training course was a bit of a shock to the system. I did it on my own with all the real recruits. I was the only actor and they quite enjoy putting you through it. It's very military – you have to march across the yard and your uniform has to be immaculate. I thought, "I'm not going to march" so I ambled across and this guy bawled me out.'

'"What do you think you're doing, you 'orrible little sod? March!"

I pleaded: "I'm in *London's Burning*."

And he laughed his head off because he had not realised.

'They're really hard on the recruits. It's the idea that they train them up to such a point and when they get on the fire station, they can then relax down but they've still got all the knowledge. You see the qualified firefighters at work and you think they're just like a bunch of lads having a laugh. You think: "How can this lot do anything?" But I spent two nights at Peckham Fire Station and when they're called out, it's serious. The banter stops straight away. They're like a slick machine.'

Stephen is not ashamed to admit that he can be rather like Colin. 'I'm a bit like him in that I'm gullible but I hope I'm more intelligent. Colin is lovable but he tries too hard. He has always wanted to be a fireman, it is his dream come true and he wants to impress everybody and be the best. He is very romantic about firefighting. He loves the idea of saving people's lives. His heart is in the right place and if he just thought a bit more before rushing into action, he would be fine.'

Reporting for duty on a dilapidated moped that looked about as effective a mode of transport as a spacehopper, Colin was a natural target for ridicule. He was incredibly naive, fresh out of training school. The first time he took hold of a water hose and tried to put out a fire, he nearly blew himself and his colleagues to kingdom come. After that, he was the butt of every station joke. The Watch told him that Tate was a born-again Christian so Colin said grace before each meal, they made him test the air for radio-active particles and even had him standing in the yard at night to test whether the luminous jackets really glowed in the dark. His fireman uncle Jaffa must have despaired of him.

And Stephen found himself on the wrong end of a few practical jokes from the cast. 'The best joke they played on me was about my size. I was a bit paranoid about my weight and, with the television cameras adding a couple of pounds, I was worried about the way I would look. I made the mistake of mentioning it to someone and gradually people kept commenting on the fact I was looking a bit plump.

'It was really underplayed and I fell for it completely. Especially when I got a letter from Paul Knight, the producer, saying that he had seen the early rushes and that he was really pleased with my performance, except that I looked a bit fat and suggested that I did some rigorous training.

'I got really worried – and when the cameraman told me to hold my stomach in during one scene, that was it! I wondered why everybody was laughing. I assumed they just thought I looked funny playing a scene with my stomach sucked in. Fortunately I got wise to the jokes before long.

'Colin's not as naive as he used to be either, now that he's proved himself a bit. He's still so enthusiastic that he leaves himself open to wind-ups but he's beginning to learn a bit more about life. He has to start doing things right otherwise he'd never get through his probation.'

Stephen, 27, likes living away from London. 'One of the good things about living in Brighton is that a lot of my friends aren't actors – I'm not particularly interested in that actory scene. It keeps you down to earth. Some of my mates are on the dole, some work in shops and just because I'm in this, I'm no different. They don't make a big thing of me being in London's Burning.'

Away from *London's Burning*, Stephen is an active member of the Labour Party and a music freak. 'I've got a big record collection – everything from classical to way-out modern jazz including Sixties soul, acid house, the lot. I'm an old punk at heart.

'I was in a band and the undoubted highlight of my life so far was when my band, Turn Of Vice, supported The Damned at Oxford College of Further Education in 1982. Funnily enough their outrageous leader, Captain Sensible, lives in Brighton and I met him in a pub last year and told him I once supported him. We had a good chat about the old punk days.'

What on earth would Colin have thought?

Sicknote is only half the man he used to be – and that has nothing to do with one of his ailments. When Les Murphy was relaying his Brigade experiences to Jack Rosenthal prior to the creation of the initial *London's Burning* film, he described a fireman he knew at a station in North London. But this man was so unbelievable that Jack had to split him into two characters – Sicknote and Charisma.

'This person not only used to swing the lead like Sicknote,' says Richard Walsh, 'but he also imagined he was Jack the Lad, the way Charisma did. He led this Walter Mitty life. But Jack Rosenthal decided that nobody would believe such a character on television so he split him in two.'

Richard believes there are people like Sicknote in all walks of life. 'Lots of people stop me in the street and say there's somebody just like Sicknote in their office. He's been in the Fire Brigade a long time, the best part of 20 years, so he is experienced and, in terms of firefighting ability, as good as anybody. But because of his character and in the way he relates to the Watch, he seems a bit pompous. He takes himself far too seriously.

'On the one hand, he's a pain in the backside and therefore the butt of a lot of their jokes but also when they want something done, they know they can get him to do it, because he has got great organisational ability. Besides no one else ever wants to do it. So in fact they're quite pleased to let him – it shelves the responsibility and anyway the organising ability of the others is absolutely nil.

'He doesn't mind doing the good works but he likes to be appreciated. However they're an ungrateful bunch of sods so they don't say thanks and he takes umbrage.'

Sicknote's major storyline in the fourth series was when he stood for the Green Party in the local elections. But after a successful campaign, he quickly found the burden of being a councillor too much to bear. 'Events overtook him rather,' says Richard. 'It started with a city farm closing down and he took that on board because his kids suppos-edly used to go to this farm. He is the sort of person who would bother to photocopy all those letters and would bother going round pushing all the leaflets through letterboxes. As I say, there are Sicknotes all over the country.

'The pompous side of Sicknote has developed as the series have gone on but he's not as much of a hypochondriac as he used to be. There's the occasional "Oh, me legs" as he goes up a ladder. But if anyone else has got any aches and pains, he knows the remedy – he remembers from his hypochondriac days. I treat Sicknote seriously because I don't think he can be funny unless he's serious. If you tried to make him funny, you'd lose it all.'

The other facet of Sicknote's character that has grown is his interest in amateur dramatics as a dedicated member of the Penge Occasional Players.

'When we were doing the original film,' says Richard, 'Paul Knight was sussing people out about their background, looking for anything that might be useful if it went to a series, and I told him I used to do amateur dramatics. I told him about the petty warfare that goes on in those societies. Although I was born in Lewisham in South-East London, I spent a lot of my schooldays in Tunbridge Wells and that's the headquarters of drama queens. They were unbelievable – the way they wore cravats, called each other "lovey" and "dahling" and always used to leave a little bit of make-up on when they came into the bar afterwards. It was more theatrical than anything I've ever been in. I've done rep. and I've appeared in six West End shows but I've never seen anything like that.

'Every night one of them would say, "There's someone from the BBC in tonight." There never was – it was just a way of geeing you up. All the girl stage assistants used to wear long men's shirts and fishnet tights because they thought that's what they wore in the West End. They were more made-up than anybody else and they weren't even on stage.

'The size of the parts you got depended on how many years you had been with the society – it didn't matter a jot whether you were right for it. I remember seeing a 40-year-old woman playing Dorothy in *The Wizard Of Oz*! I tended to play a lot of street urchins.'

Acting runs in Richard's family. His grandmother was a member of the famous D'Oyly Carte Opera Company and his father's cousin, Fred Kitchen, was in vaudeville, a member of Fred Karno's Army. 'He was quite famous,' says Richard. 'He even got a few lines in Charlie Chaplin's autobiography.

'I was a natural performer as a child. I'm one of a family of five and if people came round to our house you had to get up on a chair and recite something, they didn't have to force me much. I loved it.' Richard also developed a taste for light opera and appeared in Gilbert and Sullivan productions at the Skinner School, Tunbridge Wells, a seat of education which boasts actor Alec McCowen as one of its former pupils. After studying at RADA, Richard made his professional debut in *Julius Caesar* at Theatre Clwyd, Mold. 'I did 40 weeks rep in Wales to earn my Equity card. It was the only theatre I've worked in with cows outside the stage door.

'Prior to *London's Burning*, my only experience of the Fire Brigade was as a kid at our home in Lewisham when we had chimney fires. They used to come in, put the fire out, clonk through in their boots, have a cup of tea and go off again. But I never had any ambition to drive a fire engine which is odd since I do it a lot these days. Mind you, we rarely drive them on the open road and when we do, there's always a qualified instructor somewhere in the cab.'

Richard is only too aware that the actors have to be as safety-conscious as real firefighters. 'For instance, it's important to keep your helmet on,' he says. 'I learned that the hard way after filming a house fire. The heat was so intense it melted the guttering and molten lead dripped on to my coat. It was inches away from my head.

'I think *London's Burning* is never as good as when it's all about fighting fires. That's why episodes nine and ten of the fourth series were so strong because the soap element stemmed from our firefighters being trapped. It would be wrong to have people emerge unscathed from every shout, both physically and mentally. You talk about babies being burned and old people going up in flames and it's terribly sad. The public don't see it but firefighters see an awful lot of it. These are very brave men and women.'

Richard, 39, is married and lives in West London from where he pursues his twin hobbies of cricket and horse racing. 'I love cricket and play for the National Theatre team. I bowl medium pace, seam up and bat very badly. If there was a number 12, I'd probably bat there. I'm the ferret – I go in after the rabbits! Playwright David Hare turns out for us occasionally, so does Roger Lloyd Pack who plays Trigger in *Only Fools and Horses*. And Michael Bryant used to umpire for us.

'I've loved horse racing since I was a kid and my father discovered the *Sporting Life* in my satchel when I was 12. He beat me soundly round the ears and said, "Don't let me ever see you with that again."'

Seasoned actor James Hazeldine reckons the main thing he has in common with Bayleaf is food. But even then the similarity is not too deep. Whereas in his role as mess manager at Blackwall, Bayleaf specialises in sturdy stews, James's palate is slightly more refined.

'One of my real passions is cooking,' says James. 'I enjoy it because it's so relaxing and it gives me a chance to experiment. I love going out to buy food and then preparing it. Nowhere could I indulge myself more than when I lived for a time in New York. I was on Broadway for about six months playing Glenda Jackson's husband in the play *Strange Interlude*. I ate out all the time. Down in Greenwich Village there were lots of good places, from Mexican to French to Italian. One of my special memories is of finding a Jewish delicatessen and also an Italian one. I was like a kid in fairyland because there was a range of meats and foods you wouldn't believe possible under one roof. Alas, I've never done anything more on *London's Burning* than chop onions.'

Born in Salford, James's childhood ambition was to be a film director. His hero at the time was Elia Kazan who directed *On the Waterfront* with Brando and *East of Eden* with James Dean. 'Kazan began as an actor then became a director and that's what I wanted to do.'

James started out in repertory theatre, his first part being in *All Things Bright and Beautiful* by Keith Waterhouse and Willis Hall. 'I was 16 but wore a flat cap and a false moustache because the character was older. I only had one line – I had to walk across the stage and say, "Now then."'

From that humble beginning, 43-year-old James has become one of the country's most sought-after actors. He has worked with both the Royal Shakespeare Company and the National Theatre, teamed up again with Glenda Jackson for the film *Business As Usual* and has appeared in numerous television series including *Sam, One Summer, Truckers*, the situation comedies *Young, Gifted And Broke* and *Streets Apart*, the controversial play *Close Relations* and, last Christmas, *The Pirate Prince* in

which he starred with fellow Blue Watch member Sean Blowers.

'Sean and I got a lot of stick from the rest of the *London's Burning* cast. They hobbled about on crutches with parrots on their shoulders and were forever shouting "Shiver Me Timbers!" and "Yo-Ho-Ho And A Bottle Of Rum." The swashbuckling was great fun. I did my own stunts – I couldn't resist the chance to swing on ropes and have a fight with an 18th century cutlass. And I got to film in Dominica whereas poor Sean didn't get any further than South Wales – and it rained. I don't think he was too pleased to discover they had re-created the Caribbean outside Cardiff for his scenes. And just to rub salt into the wounds, I got to kill him. In truth, that's the only reason I accepted the part!'

Yet of all his varied roles, none has brought James as much attention as that of Bayleaf. 'I loved Jack Rosenthal's script – it was absolutely brilliant. *London's Burning* has given me a fascinating insight into the world of firefighters. It's the way they relieve the tension and I suppose the boredom. When we were preparing for the film, I saw them stand a dummy outside the station, dress it up in a fireman's uniform, stick a radio in it and, using a microphone from a safe vantage point, have it say some rude things to passers-by. I suppose you've got to do something when you're sat around with little to do and the next minute you may be racing to the scene of a terrible death – perhaps even your own.

'I particularly enjoyed the training course. We gelled as a group and actors are used to picking things up quickly and looking as if they know what they're doing, even if they don't.'

Bayleaf has always been the most sympathetic member of Blue Watch. When Josie arrived and was greeted with open hostility by the rest of the men, Bayleaf took her under his wing. They became friends, to the annoyance of her husband Gerry, and eventually had an ill-fated, misconceived one-night fling. At the start of *London's Burning*, Bayleaf was still grieving over the fact that his wife Karen had recently left him, taking with her their only child Melanie. He wanted them to get back together again but she would only think about it if he agreed to leave the Brigade. With his relationship with Josie going nowhere, Bayleaf became attracted to fireman's widow Clare, the mother of two boys. Melanie returned to live with him and Clare suggested they all move in together under one roof. She also wanted Bayleaf to seek a posting to the relative safety of Croydon but, much to his relief, this was turned down. Seemingly a happy family, they have recently moved into a new house.

'Bayleaf is probably the most sensible of the Watch,' says James. 'He's nice and easygoing. Although he is divorced, he is fairly happy-go-lucky and doesn't like to make a fuss about things. He also has a dry sense of humour. He has been a fireman for over 20 years. He always wanted to be a fireman and didn't really want promotion. He would be good officer material but he prefers being one of the lads.'

James's most harrowing experience on *London's Burning* was the big warehouse fire in which he was buried alive.'The sheer power and terror of fire is what I remember. When a fire is out of control, the most terrible things can happen. Even well-equipped and brave firefighters seem almost inadequate by comparison to the strength of the fire. There is only so much they can do. It was all very spectacular and dramatically exciting but I think what you are left with is a feeling of fear after filming something like that. You're not on a high, rather you're aware of what can happen in real life. I got a feeling of helplessness, if you like. They say that fire and water are our closest friends but our greatest enemies and I hope that was brought home to viewers.'

London's Burning has also given James the opportunity to make his debut at television direction. He directed an episode for the new series which featured a fire at an underground car park. 'I simply asked Paul Knight if I could direct an episode and he said, "Good idea." I think that was great of him. I've directed in the theatre before but of course this was completely different. I loved it and fortunately Bayleaf wasn't in that episode much so my dual roles didn't overlap to that great an extent. Needless to say, I got plenty of stick from the cast. Beforehand, whenever I walked in the room, they would stop talking and say, "Ssh, here comes the management."'

James lives in Oxfordshire with his wife Rebecca, son Sam, 19, and daughter Chloe, 11. Apart from directing more for television, he has another ambition – to work with Sam. James says: 'Sam's at RADA and is hoping to be an actor. When he was six or seven, I did a BBC series called *The Omega Factor* and he was in a scene kicking a ball around in a park. He knows the pitfalls of acting but let's face it there's no longer any such thing as a safe job. I look forward to appearing with him. That would be nice.'

When Samantha Beckinsale heard that she was in line for a part in *London's Burning*, she thought it was to play a dead body or a girlfriend.

'I was convinced it would be just a minor role, like a corpse or a bit of fluff because they were the parts I was getting at the time – airheads. So when I learned I was to be the new and only female firefighter, I was staggered.

'It all started with Corinne Rodriguez, the casting director on *London's Burning*, seeing me in a play about a women's volleyball team. She rang my agent one day and asked whether I could do a Geordie accent. I think if you can't do those accents really expertly, you shouldn't try because they sound awful. So I decided I wasn't going to lie and told my agent to say that I couldn't do a Geordie accent convincingly but that I was from north of Watford anyway. Corinne said, "Thanks for being honest. We'll have her in."

'That was on the Tuesday. I saw Corinne on Thursday and she asked me back on Friday to meet Paul Knight and Gerry Mill. I found out on my way home, on Nottingham station, that I'd got the part. I was to start work the following Monday. I couldn't believe it. My immediate thoughts were, "What about the washing? Where am I going to live?" – because I was absolutely skint at the time. I was six months behind with the rent on my place in Nottingham and the bank had told me to cut up my cheque card. So the job couldn't have come at a better time.'

Sam confesses that she didn't have the faintest idea what to expect on *London's Burning*. 'On that first Monday morning, they took me to the training centre and dumped me there in my uniform.' But she is in no doubt as to the moment when she knew that she would make it as a television firefighter. It was when she finally emerged unscathed from a narrow sewer.

'One of the things I had to do on the training course was go through a concrete sewer pipe. They sent me in fully rigged in breathing apparatus and I was told to hoist myself along on my elbows and then stretch one arm out in order to lessen the width of my shoulders. But I didn't listen and got stuck. It was sheer panic being stuck in this concrete tunnel and not being able to move. Through my face mask, I shouted, "Pull me out, pull me out." It was so claustrophobic.

'They pulled me out and said, "You don't have to do it again if you don't want to." But I knew if I didn't go back in that tunnel, I'd always regret it. So I did it. It was horrific and I was so glad to be out the other end.'

All in all, the training course was a fairly unforgettable experience for Sam. 'It was like an Army camp. I was exhausted every day – I was asleep by 8.30 every night. While I was there, a documentary series was showing about female firefighter Carol Harrison called *Fire!* I wanted to watch it but I couldn't keep my eyes open. And the boots crippled me to start with. They ripped the skin off the backs of my heels – I couldn't walk in them. So I studied firefighting videos for a day to let them heal a little.

'The rat run was an eye-opener too. It is a caged structure with three different levels and you have to manoeuvre with B.A. through pipes and tight holes. The B.A. was really strange at first because of the restriction of having your face covered. You have to learn to trust the fact that when you do breathe in, there is going to be air there. Sometimes you don't get it right. You breathe in and there's no air. It's horrible, real panic stations. Neither was I too happy 100ft up on the end of a turntable ladder. When you first go up, they let it rest and say, "Have a good look at the view." You relax, then they start it up and you come away from the ladder. The guy said he could see my white knuckles from the ground. Nothing could prise me off that ladder – I was like a cat. That experience means I don't bat an eyelid now when it comes to heights.'

But it was all worthwhile for at the end of the course, Sam received the ultimate accolade. 'What really made it for me was on the last day when we all went for a drink afterwards and the boys in my squad said they'd trust me with their lives. That

was the biggest compliment I could have been paid. I was really pleased.'

Sam, 25, was born in Derbyshire and studied drama at Clarendon College, Nottingham. She began by stuffing envelopes in a production office before going out on tour to earn her Equity card. 'The first time I was in front of a camera was for a programme called *Catering With Care* for Channel 4. It was part of the Open College course. It was terrifying, all improvisation showing the right and wrong way to behave in a kitchen – things like sneezing and spluttering into your hands and then buttering bread. Thankfully I didn't have to do any actual cooking.'

Further television work followed in *Shelley*, where she played a secretary, and in *Never The Twain*; where she was a policewoman. In the meantime, the bills still had to be paid and that meant Sam doing all manner of jobs. 'I've done shop demonstrations, selling mirrors, I've worked on a butcher's market stall. I'll have a go at anything. I used to work at Woolies on a Saturday when I was at school. Everyone should have a go at that.'

That get-up-and-go attitude is a trait Sam shares with Kate Stevens. 'She's quite a decisive girl,' says Sam. 'One of the reasons I like *London's Burning* is that I know I've done a day's work – it's a very physical show. Kate's a physical person too. She couldn't do an office job – she'd get fidgety. She goes for things – she's that sort of character. She's also a real party girl as well as being a very good firewoman and she can certainly hold her own with the boys.'

Sam sees no reason why more women should not be able to quickly climb the fire-service ladder. 'I think everyone has their own qualities, especially in the Fire Brigade where it's all about teamwork. So men in general are physically stronger than women but women are known to be emotionally stronger than men and it's a very stressful and emotional job. So maybe women can cope better than men on the stress side.

'When I was doing my training, there were boys on the squad who were more frightened of heights than I was or weren't as good in the B.A. as I was and there would be other things that they were better at. Firefighting is all to do with attitude. You can have all the physical attributes, do all the work, but if you haven't got the right attitude, you're not going to make it.'

The physical side of the job presents few problems for firewoman Sam. 'I grew up on a farm, baling hay and humping wood, so I've always been an outdoor girl. And I used to do weight training.'

She is not often recognised in the street because she usually wears her hair up in the show. 'I don't spend much time in make-up before filming. It only takes about 15 minutes for them to plait my hair and pile it on top of my head. They slap a little powder on for the benefit of the cameras but make-up and lacquer are banned in the Brigade because they can be a fire risk.'

'I had a great uncle who was a retained fireman,' says Valerie Holliman. 'I used to try his fireman's hat on when I was little.' Until she won the part of Bayleaf's girlfriend Clare in *London's Burning*, that distant memory was the extent of Valerie's association with the Brigade. 'I could certainly never have joined the Fire Brigade. I couldn't have coped with the heights because I suffer from vertigo.'

The new series sees Bayleaf and Clare installed in a new house, together with his daughter and her two sons. 'Clare's had her trials and tribulations,' says Valerie. 'She is a widow, her fireman husband having been killed in a car crash five years ago. Consequently, there is always a fear of dèja vu in her relationship with Bayleaf. That's why she wanted him to get a posting to Croydon – she thought it would be safer there than Blackwall. They did split up for a while when she started to get a bit naggy but she eventually backed down over Croydon. She knew he wouldn't want to move.

'She used to be a nurse so she's quite strong emotionally. She needed to be when one of her sons, Stephen, was rushed to hospital after a firework exploded in his face. And fortunately Bayleaf was around to comfort her. To her, he's the ideal man – kind, loyal and fun. And he adores the kids.'

Born in Hammersmith, Valerie spent three of her teenage years attending an English school in Rome where her father worked for the United Nations. 'I went back in 1991 with my two daughters for the first time in over 20 years and it was wonderful – it had hardly changed.'

Back in England, Valerie attended drama school and quickly made her mark in television with series such as *Tom Brown's Schooldays*, *Villains* and *Flickers*, the last two starring Bob Hoskins. 'Villains was one of the first shows Bob did. I'd never met anyone quite like him. He had so much energy and loads of ideas.'

Valerie also had the distinction of saying the first line in the final episode of *Crossroads*. 'I was in *Crossroads* for four months in all. I played Eve Maddingham, the wife of publican John. At the very end, he ran off with Jill, wife of Adam. It was funny, John and Jill went off leaving Adam with Eve!'

Her favourite episode in *London's Burning* was the charity pram race in aid of cystic fibrosis. 'It was great fun. We were all there. Samantha Beckinsale dressed up as Tweetie Pie, Rupert Baker was an old lady, Sean Blowers was a teddy boy and James Hazeldine and I went as St Trinian's girls.'

Like James Hazeldine's son Sam, Valerie's daughters are TV veterans. 'Holly, who's 16 now, was a girl dying of kidney failure in an episode of *Casualty* and when she was only five, she had six months' work playing Carolyn Pickles' daughter in LWT's wartime saga *We'll Meet Again*. The director on that was John Reardon who of course directs some of *London's Burning*. My youngest daughter Nina, who is 13, has appeared twice on screen with me. She played my daughter in an episode of *The Bill* and when she was four months old, she played my son in *The Professionals*! Well, at that age and wrapped in a shawl, it's difficult to tell whether it's a boy or a girl.'

Not a lot of people know that Tracey Ullman was once Bonnie Langford's backing singer. And even fewer people know that Amanda Dickinson used to be Tracey Ullman's backing singer.

Amanda, who plays Sicknote's long-suffering wife Jean, worked for record company EMI before touring the world with Tracey. 'It was a great time for me,' says Amanda. 'We did all the big shows – *Top of the Pops*, *The Johnny Carson Show*, *American Bandstand*, a David Frost show in Australia and the Montreux Pop Festival. I got to see the world – it was a fabulous experience.'

It's all a far cry from genteel Sittingbourne in Kent where Amanda was raised and where she began her drift into showbusiness. 'Most of my family had some sort of artistic background. My grandfather was a conductor, my mother was a drama teacher and my cousins went to drama school so I decided to follow suit. When I was 18, I also studied dancing. I really don't know why I did it because I didn't enjoy it much and I've sworn that I'll never lift my foot again. Dancing is definitely not for me.'

Amanda spent two years on tour with Tracey Ullman before concentrating on an acting career. And by a strange coincidence her television debut was in two episodes of the flat-sharing comedy series *Girls On Top* which starred Dawn French, Jennifer Saunders, Ruby Wax...and Tracey Ullman. Amanda has also appeared in *The Bill*, *Inspector Morse*, *About Face* (starring Jack Rosenthal's wife Maureen Lipman), *The Manageress*, *The Good Guys* and *The Harry Enfield Show*.

'I think Harry Enfield is wonderful,' says Amanda, 'so I was thrilled to be on his show. In fact, I'd have been quite happy just standing around doing very little. And the soccer-mad guys on *London's Burning* were particularly impressed that I'd been in *The Manageress* – I played Mandy, the crooked accountant's girl-friend.

'I love being in *London's Burning* – everyone is so friendly. But sometimes I despair of my character Jean Quigley. Poor woman, I think her life is about as exciting as watching paint dry. Sicknote's such a twerp but I suppose he must have hidden qualities otherwise she wouldn't have stayed with him all this time. Mind you, there was more than a hint of an affair with Dominic from the Penge Occasional Players. But he was another plonker! In the end, she only took Sicknote back because Dominic hurt his throat and couldn't star in The Student Prince.

'I'm afraid Jean definitely has aspirations above her station – that's why of all the wives, she gets on best with Sandra Hallam. I imagine Jean reads Hello magazine for articles like the 50 best outfits of Princess Diana. She'd like to better herself but instead she's married to this bloody idiot and belongs to this terrible amateur dramatic company.'

Fortunately Amanda's own future is far rosier, underlined by the fact that she recently completed Jack Rosenthal's latest film, *Bye Bye Baby*, about National Service. 'I played a NAAFI girl but in my hat I managed to end up looking like Su Pollard.'

Amanda is single and lives in London with three dogs and two cats. 'I adore animals and will do anything I can to help them. I really enjoyed doing the City farm scene in *London's Burning* because I got to play with the animals. I'm also a big music fan. That dates back to my three years with EMI where I used to go out and watch all manner of bands. My taste varies now according to my mood – it can be anything from opera to heavy metal band Guns N' Roses.'

Oh, and Amanda has one other passion too. 'I'm really into Sumo wrestling.' Sicknote had better watch out...

As a child, Vanessa Pett had always wanted to be a dancer but she could never have expected to trip the light fantastic on a show like *London's Burning*. Yet that is exactly what happened when Vanessa was cast as calculating Kelly, the girl who used her charms to persuade George to take up ballroom dancing. The next thing he knew, he was dancing up the aisle with Kelly claiming that she was pregnant.

'My dance training certainly came in handy,' says Vanessa. 'And although he wasn't very keen at first, Glen Murphy, who plays George, turned out to be an excellent dancing partner. There were no sore toes, I wasn't trodden on at all. He really looked good. I think his boxing background helped him with his footwork.'

Having coerced George into getting married, Kelly mentioned in the honeymoon suite that she might not be pregnant after all. Poor George felt well and truly trapped and to make matters worse, he even had to fight off the attentions of Kelly's mum who tried to seduce him while he was collecting prams for the charity race. But now Kelly definitely is pregnant.

'Kelly knew what she wanted,' says Vanessa, 'and that was George. On the outside, she's bubbly, gentle and sweet – a fluffy extrovert. But beneath all that lies a steely determination.'

Vanessa, who lives in Shepherd's Bush with her actor boyfriend Anthony, was raised in Bristol. Her parents were both stage actors and, after appearing in various school plays such as Arthur Miller's *The Crucible* when she was 13, she studied acting at the Drama Centre in London for two years. 'It was a serious method school of acting where we really had to "live" the characters for the whole day.

It was exhausting. After that, I think I was prepared for anything.'

She went on to appear in repertory at Chichester and Leeds and in television productions including *C.A.T.S Eyes, Never the Twain* and The Channel 4 film *Going Home*. Her hobbies include yoga and reading tarot cards for her friends. 'But I never tell them if it's bad news.'

Last year, she presented an environmental series for HTV entitled *Chain Reaction*. 'It was a nice change to be able to do something serious instead of playing fluffy blondes. It was certainly a contrast to Kelly. Can you imagine her presenting an environmental series? The amount of hairspray she uses has actually helped to destroy the ozone layer.'

*L*ondon's Burning fans could be forgiven for doing a double take when they see Scottish actress Ona McCracken as Recall's wife Laura. For Ona had previously played a small part in the first series of the programme as Detective Sergeant Crawford, called in to investigate the attempted rape on Josie.

Ona has certainly enjoyed a varied career, encompassing everything from corpses to pop videos.

Born in Glasgow, she started out working backstage at the local Citizens Theatre, making props, painting scenery and appearing as an extra. At 21, she decided to come to London to study at the Central School of Speech and Drama. 'I felt I had to get away from Glasgow,' explains Ona. 'I had to learn to be able to speak properly. The trouble was that not many Scots acted and all the best parts at the Citizens went to the suave and sophisticated set-up from London who were all terribly glamorous. All I ever got were beggars, tramps, punk rockers and prostitutes! It was a really daunting scene so I had to escape but it was a question of plucking up courage to do so.'

Down in London, Ona spent three years at Central and then did fringe theatre above pubs. 'I appeared in classics like *The Cherry Orchard* which I couldn't possibly have done at the RSC at my age.'

After playing a radio station receptionist in the Bill Forsyth film *Comfort and Joy*, Ona turned to pop videos. 'I did a Robert Palmer video and also one for Wham! That was mainly dancing and kissing and I never did get to meet the boys – they were kept separate from us. I also appeared in a Hitchcock spoof for a Troggs video. I played Kim Novak and had to watch all her old movies to copy that enigmatic walk. Unfortunately the song, "Every Little Thing", wasn't a hit but it was good fun to do.'

Ona has since found herself in demand for police series. 'I was a plainclothes detective sergeant who has having an affair with her superior in *The Chief*, I was a receptionist in *Van Der Valk* and a rough, pregnant mum with loads of kids in *The Bill*. I hated that because I had to smoke.

'I was also an intelligence agent/Communist/actress/cleaner in P.D. James' *A Taste For Death*. It was a very complicated part. Luckily I was murdered in the second episode!

'Mind you, it wasn't a very nice death. I drowned and it was very cold because I was nearly naked at the time. I've been a corpse in the theatre and that's fine because you can have a nice lie down but it's not as much fun on television.'

Thirty-three-year-old Ona is single and lives in Camberwell, South London. An avid Raymond Chandler fan, she still nurtures the ambition to be a female private detective. In the meantime, she'll settle for guiding her ladies' pool team to victory over the men.

Bubbly Ona has a serious side too and was deeply moved by the storyline in *London's Burning* in which Laura and Recall's son Jamie has cystic fibrosis. 'Laura has had a really tough life,' says Ona. 'It must be so difficult living under such a strain. To research the storyline, Ben Onwukwe and I met a lady from the support group South London Cystic Fibrosis. Her daughter has cystic fibrosis. She told us that she didn't know that her daughter had the disease until her lung collapsed. She said that attention to her other children just went out of the window and she explained how the whole thing put her marriage under a great strain. She gave me loads of help, things like reminding me never to cry in front of the child. You always have to smile. You are only allowed to cry when the child's not around. It certainly opened my eyes.

'So when we filmed the pram race, I was delighted that we managed to raise so much money from onlookers. I think the presence of the cameras worked in our favour though – they make people feel guilty about saying no.'

While the other members of the cast are bravely fighting raging infernos, Shirley Greenwood has no doubt about her toughest task in *London's Burning* – it was to sing badly. For unbeknown to anyone on the series, Shirley is a trained soprano with ten West End musicals to her name.

'On the very first episode I did, the director came over to me and said, "I'd like Maggie to sing. I hope you don't mind." So Maggie helped out Sicknote with his rehearsals for *There Is Nothing Like A Dame* with the Penge Occasional Players. It was difficult for me because Maggie was not supposed to be a proper singer. So I tried to sing badly, shouting like you would in a pub. It was ironic to say the least.'

Kindly Maggie works in the mess kitchen at Blackwall. 'I've been told by firefighters,' says Shirley, 'that a real Maggie would be the pivot of the station. Anyone with marital problems would immediately go to her. She's like a surrogate mother to them all, a good listener.

'At first, she was something of a dark horse – she was supposed to have done a singing double act in cabaret with her husband Albert. But Albert's only been seen once, at Vaseline's funeral. The only time he's ever talked about now is when I mention my Bert's prostate! Maggie's daughter is unseen too although we do know that she works for an airline company because it was she who got the free tickets for Recall and Laura to take little Jamie to Florida.'

Clapham-born Shirley was late getting into showbusiness professionally. She did amateur dramatics but was basically too busy raising three children – Deborah, now 33, who is a potter, Jeremy, 30, who works in advertising, and Annabel, 27, a singer who co-incidentally lives virtually next door to the studios where *London's Burning* is filmed.

Shirley's first professional job was as principal girl singing in pantomime with Cyril Fletcher at Cambridge. 'I didn't tell anyone I was going in for the audition. Then when I got the part, I nearly had kittens. I thought it was going to be in London and I had the problem of finding someone to collect the children from school.'

Shirley went on to appear in *Two Cities* with Edward Woodward and *Passionella* with Danny La Rue. She toured the country as Snow White, played Dr Dolittle's landlady Mrs Hopkins in *My Fair Lady* at the Adelphi Theatre for two and a half years and, also at the Adelphi, played Marilyn Monroe's mother's nurse in the production of *Marilyn*.

But after years of musicals, Shirley decided she wanted a change and went to the Actors' Centre to learn improvisation. 'I had always wanted to act but because you're a singer, they don't take you seriously. Anyway I did fringe theatre for no money but luckily Corinne Rodriguez saw me. So it brought me *London's Burning*. I still do the occasional musical though. Last year I was in the Royal Command Performance of *My Fair Lady* and was fortunate enough to meet The Queen.'

At 56, Shirley has another string to her bow too – she can frequently be found serving behind the counter of her family shop. 'When my husband Stan was made redundant from his job as a design engineer, we opened up a little gift shop in Forest Hill, South London. We've had it for six years now and we sell things like cards, glassware and jewellery. It's nice – I particularly enjoy the buying. It also means that I no longer have to accept any old theatre part that comes along.

'It's not our first business venture. We used to run a bistro in Forest Hill – next door to where we are now.

'I love cookery and throw plenty of dinner parties. That's another thing I find hard about playing Maggie – some of the food she has to prepare. I have to be seen making these awful cheese sandwiches although fortunately the props boys make them beforehand unless the camera is actually on me. And I remember when we did the Christmas Special, the smell of those brussel sprouts cooking in the studio all day made me feel ill.

'Even so, I do not envy Blue Watch hanging around in the cold or up to their waists in water. I like my kitchen.'

Who would ever have thought from watching Helen Blizard as Vaseline's downtrodden widow Marion that she once starred on *Top of the Pops*? And she owed it all to a lousy cup of tea.

As a young drama student, to make ends meet Helen worked as a waitress in a fish and chip shop at Crawley, Sussex, and one day found herself serving Rocky Sharpe and his brother from the Fifties' revival group Rocky Sharpe and the Razors. 'They complained so bitterly about the quality of the tea,' remembers Helen, 'that they almost got me the sack. I went over and told them that there was nothing wrong with my tea and how they had nearly got me fired and then we got chatting. After that, I started going to their shows whenever I could.

'While I was studying at Bristol Old Vic, Rocky Sharpe and the Razors split up. Half went off to form The Darts and the three remaining guys asked me if I wanted to join them in a new group, Rocky Sharpe and the Replays. In 1978, we released a song called *Rama Lama Ding Dong* and it reached number 17 in the charts. After years of tuning in to *Top of the Pops*, I suddenly found myself appearing on it. I think we were all a bit shell-shocked by the whole experience.

'I managed to combine my studies with my singing and we toured Britain and made TV appearances in Germany, Italy and Spain. We were pretty big in Spain. I stayed with them for four years in all and we had a few hairy moments. Once we were booked to do a television show in Italy but when we arrived, we discovered that we were supposed to be singing a different song from the one we had been rehearsing. So we had to frantically rehearse a new number in the toilets before going on!'

Following her final doo-wop, Helen made her TV acting debut back in England as a punk girl in the popular children's series *Metal Mickey*. She then starred as a luckless bride in Yorkshire Television's *Glorious Day*. 'It was so cold filming at this hill-top church in Leeds that I had to have hot-water bottles under my wedding dress.'

Last year, Helen played Del Boy's old girl-friend Trudie in *Only Fools and Horses*. 'Trudie was drunk and disorderly and very loud – a total embarrassment to Del Boy,' says Helen. 'What with Marion, I hope this doesn't mean I'm becoming too closely identified with playing volatile young women.'

Most of Helen's work has been with London fringe theatre where she has earned considerable acclaim from such productions as *A Streetcar Named Desire*, *Ernest, Scott and Zelda* and *Flare Path*, the last two earning her nominations for Best Actress on the Fringe. It was while playing Cindy in *Like A Fish Needs A Bicycle* at the King's Head that she was spotted by *London's Burning* casting director Corinne Rodriguez.

'Marion is a challenging role for any actress,' says Helen. 'I suppose she is one of life's victims. She has been in a difficult situation – Vaseline's death left her living on the breadline with no money and a baby. She's not trained to earn her own living and anyway she simply hasn't got the confidence. She rants and raves a lot but inside she knows she is powerless to do anything about her problems.'

It was only when Vaseline's first wife, Marion one, came to stay (leading to Vaseline's lament, 'Marion three thinks I'm giving Marion one one too') that she gained in confidence. Helen continues: 'She was finally beginning to get the strength to leave Vaseline, to be rid of his womanising, when he died. And that really set her back. She was flattered by the attentions of Technique but was too naive to see through him. She treated Kevin badly and then tried to commit suicide.

'It was hard doing the suicide bid because we filmed it at about 8 o'clock in the morning. I had to try to think of something depressing to get me in the mood. It's easier when Marion has to be angry – I just think of rude people, injustice or even the tax man!'

Picture the scene. A tense moment in the Hallam household. The tarpaulin covering the space where Sandra's kitchen window should be has blown on to a neighbouring roof. Outside, the Hallams – John, Sandra and the two children – appraise the situation. What the camera doesn't show is that young daughter Lillian is perched on a brick and Sandra is standing on a box!

Kim Clifford laughs: 'It's the problem of Sean Blowers being 6 ft. 1in., the little girl who plays Lillian being tiny and me being only 5 ft. 3 in. He's not going to shrink so we have to be made taller. It's really funny to see us doing it. Eat your heart out, Alan Ladd.

'For the last series, I was pregnant too, expecting baby Jack, so I had to wear flat shoes. Even when I sat on a chair, there had to be a box underneath. Not only was I always shot from the waist up, but I had to be constantly carrying baskets of washing to hide my bulge.'

As if it's not enough having one fireman husband, Kim has two. For her real spouse is actor-turned-fireman Lee Galpin. The former member of the National Youth Theatre joined the London Fire Brigade three years ago and, in the finest tradition of Brigade nicknames, was immediately christened Sir Larry.

Lee reckons London's Burning is largely true to life and he has always been a big fan of the series although it wasn't that which inspired him to join the Brigade. He had already worked for the St John Ambulance and wanted another job which served the community. 'It was handy when he was doing his training,' says Kim. 'I was able to help him study for his exams because through London's Burning, I knew all the terminology.'

Born in Islington, Kim joined Anna Scher's children's drama school and appeared in countless Saturday morning films for the Children's Film Foundation. When she was 13, she played the only non-Jew in Jack Rosenthal's highly-acclaimed Bar Mitzvah Boy. 'I had the opening line. It was "You lying bugger, you did." It was a great opening line although a bit daring for a 13-year-old. Fortunately my mum and dad saw the funny side.'

Kim, who also appeared in Jack Rosenthal's film The Chain, specialised in playing schoolgirls and teenagers in shows like Not The Nine O'Clock News, Alas – Smith and Jones and Juliet Bravo. 'Now on screen I've got a husband and two children. I've gone through professional puberty on London's Burning.'

At 31, Kim is one day younger than TV husband Sean Blowers. 'We're terrible gigglers,' confesses Kim. 'When John had been away on a course and Sandra was furiously jealous, I had to throw his Y-fronts at him when he returned. It was so hard to keep a straight face that I kept throwing them and hitting the cameras. Some of the scenes do get to me though. When we were all called out early one morning on a very cold day to film the funeral of Vaseline, played by Mark Arden, we were all really downcast. I came home that night and saw Mark advertising Carling Black Label. It seemed eerie.'

What does the naturally effervescent Kim think of the dreaded Sandra? 'Sandra is the poison dwarf of Blue Watch but I'm glad she has been shown to be a bit human now. For a lot of the last series, I seemed to be standing with arms folded and a furrowed brow. All the business of the kitchen was a case of reflected power. Because John is a sub-officer, she feels she has a position to maintain with the other wives.

'Although she's a bit of a battleaxe, Sandra does love John and she worries about him. I go through the same with Lee. He comes home and I'll say, "Did you have a good day?" And he'll say, "Yes, we went to this great fire." The thing with firemen is that a good blaze is a working day to them. To me, it's a nightmare.

'Of course, Lee takes a lot of stick from the guys at work about Sandra but they're very good whenever I meet them – they never swear in front of me. I think they reckon there's a bit of Sandra in me but I hope there isn't. They ask Lee: "Is she really like Sandra?" Lee says, "No, she's worse..."'

Gerard Horan felt the adrenalin pumping when Whitechapel Red Watch asked him to put out a fire all by himself. 'It wasn't much of a fire, just a sapling that some kids on an estate had set alight. But as we pulled up, the lads on the Watch turned to me and said, "You can do this one, Gerry. We've got some specialised equipment." I thought it would be some new invention or a fancy hose, at any rate the real McCoy, but instead they handed me a bucket of water. And that was it. What a let down. I put the fire out with one bucket. And they didn't even bother getting off the appliance!'

Gerry was visiting Whitechapel for his station experience following the training course. 'I was amazed at their bravery,' he says. 'It is very physical work as well as emotionally demanding. And there's no hanging around when they get to a fire. They just grab a hose and go in – they don't wait for anybody else to turn up and have a chat about how they're going to tackle it. For me, the best bit was definitely riding on the appliances.'

Charisma wanted the rest of the boys at Blackwall to believe he was a real Jack the Lad. In fact, the average Trappist monk had a wilder social life. And when he did find himself a girlfriend, Donna, he couldn't get rid of her.

'He was basically lonely,' says Gerry. 'But people liked him because there are Charismas in all walks of life. The writers and I had to tread a fine line with him. I didn't overdo it – I didn't want him to appear a prat or to be too cuddly. He still had to be a good fireman otherwise they'd have thrown him out.'

Born in Stockport, Gerry moved to Gloucester at the age of 18 months. He attended an all boys' school where once a year girls from the local convent took part in a play. 'Suddenly acting appealed to me,' he laughs. 'Yes, I would say that those school plays with the convent girls were definitely instrumental in the Muse landing on my shoulder.'

But before getting his big acting break, he worked as a labourer, painter and decorator and in the postroom of a legal firm with showbusiness connections. 'I spent most of the time travelling round London on the Tube delivering things by hand like the deeds to Duran Duran's new house.'

The RADA-trained actor gained invaluable experience with London's Royal Court Theatre. 'In only my second part, I went to New York with Brian Cox for a production of *Rat In The Skull*. I thought that was how it was always going to be – plenty of trips abroad.'

He went on to appear in *The Singing Detective* as Reginald, in three episodes of *Brookside* as union activist Martin Cox investigating asbestosis in Bobby Grant's factory, and of course *London's Burning*. He also teamed up with Kenneth Branagh and Emma Thompson for *Look Back In Anger* at the Lyric Theatre. After two series, he left *London's Burning* to go on a world tour with Kenneth Branagh. 'We did *King Lear* and *A Midsummer Night's Dream* and went to places like Los Angeles, Tokyo, Portugal, Hungary, Czechoslovakia. It was a once in a lifetime experience. I'd seen Bermondsey and Rotherhite on *London's Burning* so I thought I'd broaden my horizons!'

Gerry, who is 30 and single, has been kept very busy ever since, both in the theatre and in numerous television series, among them *Casualty, Boon, The Ruth Rendell Mysteries* and *Lovejoy*.

'I also played Rosencrantz in a radio version of *Hamlet*, produced by the Renaissance Theatre Company for the BBC. There was an amazing cast – Sir John Gielgud, Kenneth Branagh, Derek Jacobi, Dame Judi Dench, Sir Michael Hordern. In fact at the readthrough, I was the only person I didn't recognise!'

Charisma would have claimed to be on first-name terms with them all.

Any police officer witnessing Mark Arden's first drive in a fire appliance could have been forgiven for thinking: 'I bet he drinks Carling Black Label.'

For on Mark's own admission, he drove as if he was definitely the worse for wear. 'It was all a misunderstanding,' says Mark. 'I'd got a temporary HGV licence so that I could drive the fire appliance on *London's Burning*. The first time I went out in it was along Jamaica Road in South East London. I had to drive and talk, which can be difficult for actors, and the cab was packed. The cameraman was on my shoulder, the director was down by the pedals and the rest of the cast were in the back feeding me my lines.

'I drove like an imbecile. I didn't give way at roundabouts, I was very aggressive. We reached the end and I pulled over, really pleased with myself. And the director said, "Fine, but the trouble is you're coming BACK from a shout." I thought the sequence was on the way to a shout – that's why I was going like crazy. So I had to do it all again at a sedate 35 mph!'

Mark believes he got the role of Vaseline by auditioning at a wedding. 'I was at the wedding of Ade Edmondson and Jennifer Saunders, and Les Blair, who directed the first *London's Burning* film, was there too. I chatted away to him and I think I must have somehow convinced him of my acting skills because nine months later I was playing Vaseline.

'People considered Vaseline to be an amiable sort of bloke but they tend to forget that in the original film he was a nasty bit of work – sexist and racist. But gradually all that was toned down and he became a typically lovable British rogue with a penchant for wives called Marion. He was definitely the Marion kind...

'When it came to filming his funeral, I wanted to play a black joke on everyone. I tried to work out how I could actually get to be in the coffin for the funeral scene but it would have meant getting up at some unearthly hour. Watching it on TV was odd though – somehow I felt a bit removed from it all.'

Far from having three wives like Vaseline, Mark, 36, is single and lives on a houseboat on the Thames with his two dogs, Herbs and Finnegan. 'They're both ex-Battersea Dogs' Home mongrels,' says Mark. 'Finnegan has actually appeared on stage with me. I was doing a comedy revue called *The Wow Show* and part of it was a circus send-up. I had Finnegan come on and the moment the audience saw that it was a real dog, they all went "Aaah". Finnegan responded by wandering to the side of the stage and weeing up the curtain, to a huge round of applause.'

The Wow Show is just one of Mark Arden's many off-beat roles. Raised in South London, he trained at the Guildhall School of Music and Drama and spent four years touring Britain in repertory theatre. In 1980, he teamed up with Stephen Frost, whom he had met at the Guildhall, to form a comedy double act called The Oblivion Boys. The next few years saw them performing on the blossoming cabaret circuit and becoming regular performers at the Comedy Store and similar venues throughout London. They played a variety of roles in the frantic TV comedy *The Young Ones* and appeared on *Carrott's Lib, Blackadder, Saturday Live* and several *Comic Strip* programmes. Last year, the pair starred in their own series as inept cops Lazarus and Dingwall.

But it is the Carling Black Label lager commercials for which they have become best known. 'We started doing the ads in 1987 and they have done us a real favour,' admits Mark.

'Even though I've never managed to get on any exotic locations with the ads, I've been lucky to be associated with such good commercials. They've certainly caught on with the public. Sometimes people call out to me in the street, "Oi, Vaseline, I bet you drink Carling Black Label." It's funny, whilst I've always known the power of the ads, I didn't realise how popular Vaseline was until after he'd died.'

'Okay,' said Firefighter Josie Ingham as she bunked down for her first night in the dormitory with the sceptical male members of Blue Watch. 'Here we go. One – I'm not a dyke. Two – I'm not a women's libber. Three – I'm not a nymphomaniac. Four – I'm not an alien from Outer Space. I'm in the job because I like it. I'm not clever enough to be a nurse or a secretary. But two days and two nights a week, I'm bloody good at fighting fires.'

Actress Katharine Rogers was acutely aware of the fact that, as Josie, she was speaking for the small but growing band of women firefighters everywhere. 'One of the things that was very important to me,' says Katharine, 'was my sense of responsibility to women in the Fire Brigade. We were very careful not to precipitate any myths about women firefighters so we didn't have Josie leaping into bed with the men because one of the myths about the Brigade is that women only join to sleep with men. We aimed to show what a woman can do rather than what she can't. And I know that *London's Burning* did have an immediate effect on the way in which women in the Brigade were treated. Following the bath scene in the original film, I know that the next day at least two firewomen suddenly had baths run for them.

'When we started, I know that the majority of the population had no idea that there were women in the Fire Brigade. People said to me, "What do you do?" I replied, "The same as the men." They were absolutely amazed.'

As the only woman among a horde of men, Katharine's situation on *London's Burning* ran parallel to that of Josie. 'I was in a similar position to Josie, being the only actress in the cast and with a predominantly male crew. For the first year, people like the props guys were always offering to help me with anything physical. It was very nice of them but it was simply because I was a girl. On filming, if I tripped over a length of hose, everybody noticed but if one of the men did it, nobody batted an eyelid. Like Josie, I felt I was always being watched, constantly having to prove myself.'

Katharine and Josie took most of it in their stride. 'They told me after my training that they would accept me in the Fire Brigade,' says Katharine. 'The only really anxious time I can remember was for an episode when Josie, being the lightest in the Watch, had to climb across a burning beam in a house to rescue a man trapped on the other side. I didn't do the actual crawling but I did have to stand in a small piece of burning floor with heavy breathing apparatus. I did it three times but by the fourth "take", I'd started to lose my "bottle" and I said, "I can't do it again, I'm too nervous." As long as you're confident about these things, you can do them but once you start to get nervous, forget it.

'I also used to worry about our gas cylinders exploding. We'd be told, "Whatever you do, don't drop your B.A. cylinders" but I'd be banging my way through buildings, knocking them around. So that was a bit dodgy.'

One of Josie's most powerful storylines was when she was the victim of an attempted rape. 'I know it's a real cliche but people did come up to me in supermarkets after it was screened and say how real and horrible and messy it was. It wasn't sexual. That's not what rape is about. It's about violence and that's the point we tried to make.'

So the burning question is, why did Katharine want to leave the series? 'I left because Josie's story was basically she came, she saw, she conquered. We'd done that and I felt that there was nowhere else to go with the character. But I did want her to be promoted and move on, not married or killed off. I like to think she'll end up as a Station Officer.

'The other reason I left was because I didn't want to be trapped in a long-running series after which nobody will touch you with a 10ft barge-pole. I wanted to show I could do other things, particularly in the theatre. The money might not be great but I've got no kids so the only responsibilities I have are to myself.'

Tony Sanders and Treva Etienne have one major thing in common – they both quit Blue Watch to set up in business. Tony, drifting apart from wife Dorothy, teamed up with old school-friend Jenny to run her designer clothes and jewellery shop while Treva left to form his own production company, Crown Ten.

'Tony's ambitions extended beyond just being a fireman,' says Treva. 'The job gave him the courage to try other things. It's the same with me. I had three and a half great years on *London's Burning* but I simply wanted to do something else for a while.'

Even when he was with *London's Burning*, Treva ran his own London-based theatre

company, Afro-sax, which aimed to take theatre into the community, playing at local halls and giving work to young people. 'Crown Ten is really the successor to Afro-sax. We have a team of 26 writers and we're making comedy and drama to reflect Britain in the Nineties. We want to increase black representation on UK television and catch up with US television which is leaps and bounds ahead in terms of its portrayal of blacks. We are not trying to develop exclusive black programmes, we aim to create new ideas that show the integration of black Britain.

'And we're still doing work with kids in the community. We've held arts workshops attended by stars from programmes like *EastEnders*, *Brookside*, *Desmond's* and *The Paradise Club*. We try to help kids to communicate because you need skills like that if you're going to survive. You could have 10 "O" Levels and still not be able to communicate and you lose jobs if you can't get on with people.'

Treva, who was born in North London, left school at 15 and tried his hand at a variety of jobs. 'I worked in a fast food restaurant, sold ice cream and did a year at college studying electronics. I then worked in a metalwork factory for a day but I couldn't stand it – it was soul-destroying. All the time, I was acting in amateur and youth theatre

productions and I really only took all these jobs because I was too young to get into drama school.'

Treva holds the British record as the youngest ever Macbeth to grace the National Theatre, at the age of 21. He toured America in a production of *Measure For Measure* and has appeared in numerous television series including *The Lenny Henry Show*, *Grange Hill*, *The Paradise Club* and *Casualty*. 'On the strength of *London's Burning*, I also appeared on *Hale & Pace* playing a fireman who had to rescue a cat from a tree.'

Despite his hectic life as a writer/producer, Treva still finds time to act. He played a vicar in last year's *Only Fools and Horses Christmas Special* and has also been in a comedy sketch show, *Squash TV*.

Tony Sanders faced a dilemma familiar to all too many firefighters – lack of money, a situation exacerbated by his wife Dorothy's extravagant spending sprees. The last straw in their relationship was when Dorothy, in an effort to raise money, got a job as a hostess at a night club. Tony was furious at the prospect of her being ogled by men all evening.

Treva sympathises with the plight of firemen. 'Firefighters do a fantastic job – we'd all be lost without them. And I think one of the good things about *London's Burning* is that it allows them to respect their job. And that can't be a bad thing.'

It was a meeting with Roy Marsden, best known as TV detective Adam Dalgliesh, that led James Marcus to abandon a life in printing for acting. 'I spent my teenage years in South London,' says James, 'dabbling in rock and roll, playing in pub gigs, before going on to become an apprentice printer. I passed my indentures and was somewhat reluctantly beginning a career in printing while harbouring a dream of becoming an actor.

'But I didn't really know how to go about it. My wife's sister is married to Roy Marsden's brother so I asked Roy what I should do. He told me to go to drama school and at the age of 24, I successfully applied to the East 15 Drama School.'

James hasn't looked back since. He has made numerous television appearances, ranging from that of a policeman who tried to get the better of Martin Shaw in *The Professionals*, to John in *Jane Eyre*. He has also cropped up in *The Sweeney*, *The Naked Civil Servant*, *The Chinese Detective* and *Minder*. 'I worked on a *Minder* special, playing a character called Morrie Myers who was trying to unload a lorry load of suspect electrical goods onto Arthur Daley.'

On the big screen, James has appeared in *The Virgin Soldiers*, *A Clockwork Orange*, *McVicar* and Les Blair's *Number One*, in which he had to demand money with menaces from Bob Geldof. He also co-wrote and directed the film *Tank Malling* which starred *London's Burning's* Glen Murphy and former boxer John Conteh and told the story of investigative reporter John 'Tank' Malling.

'It was my debut as a feature film director and I found it extremely challenging. It exhausted every particle of my being but it was also very rewarding.'

Despite ailing health which ultimately led to his enforced retirement at the end of third series, Sidney Tate was the kindly father-figure of Blackwall. He even tolerated Colin. One of his most memorable storylines involved a handicapped boy, Paul, who came to spend Christmas with Tate and his wife Nancy.

James, who is married with one son Gareth, actually discovered eight-year-old Paul Carter when he visited a special school in Luton. 'My wife and I performed an opening ceremony at the school,' says James, 'and we were so captivated by Paul that I thought about including him in the story. The Tates were warm-hearted and childless and so it seemed likely that they would take in a boy over Christmas. The following day writer Tony Hoare went up to meet Paul and he too was won over.'

Paul was born with half limbs and had never acted before but gave a memorable performance. 'I had a wonderful response from people about that,' says James. 'Paul made such an impact. And he loved the fireman's helmet we presented to him on the set. I still write to him now and he's a very brainy lad.'

James, 50, now combines acting with writing and producing. He has co-written and co-produced the upcoming *Passing Through,* a film comedy about a motorway service station, and a stage play for 1993, *Family Tree*.

Yet one role returns to haunt him – that of the long-suffering Bert Banford in the Clive Dunn comedy series *Grandad*. 'Only last year, I was on my way back from Athens and the plane was diverted and didn't land till 5 am. It had been a long flight, I was really tired and in need of a good shower. Then suddenly at the airport, a group of teenagers shouted, "Oi, it's that geezer from *Grandad*!" It seems there's no escape from Bert.'

4 THE STORY SO FAR...

ORIGINAL SCREENPLAY
Writer: Jack Rosenthal
Director: Les Blair
Duration: 120 minutes
Transmission date: 7 December 1986

Garry McDonald as the hapless Ethnic.

With the exception of Bayleaf, the members of Blue Watch react with uniform hostility to the arrival at Blackwall of firewoman Josie Ingham. But she earns their respect during an emergency call to a block of flats by refusing to be flustered at the sight of a man with a curtain ring wedged on an embarrassing part of his body. More serious problems follow, first when a child is killed in a house fire and then when a young black firefighter Ethnic, on the eve of his promotion to Leading Fireman in another division, becomes embroiled in a ghetto riot between blacks and the police. As Blue Watch fight the raging fires, Ethnic rescues Charisma from being attacked by a gang of blacks – but at the cost of his own life. For another gang witness Ethnic's actions from nearby flats and launch a paving stone down on to him, killing him outright. The Watch eat in silence the feast they had prepared to celebrate Ethnic's promotion.

Series One

EPISODE ONE
Writer: Tony Hoare
Director: John Reardon
Duration: 120 minutes
Transmission date: 20 February 1988

After rescuing a boy's pet cat from a roof, Blue Watch accidentally run over the animal in their appliance, killing it. They then attend a warehouse fire where Vaseline is seriously hurt when his boots catch fire. An old tramp who has been dossing in the basement burns to death but his cat survives. The Watch take the animal to the boy to replace the one they had crushed earlier. Meanwhile they raise £1,200 for charity by pushing an antique fire engine through the streets...but then Tate discovers the money has gone missing and the police are called in. The Watch are summoned to an incident in which raiders have cemented a wealthy young City dealer into the bowl of his lavatory. Unable to release him, the firemen can hardly contain themselves as he is carried, still cemented to the lavatory bowl, to a waiting ambulance. The next shout is to a major road crash caused by a lonely, depressed old lady deliberately walking out into a busy main road in front of a lorry. New recruit Kevin panics when he finds a child trapped in the back of one of the crushed cars and Sicknote really is ill on discovering, amidst all the carnage and confusion, the old lady's severed head. On the domestic front, tongues are wagging over Bayleaf's relationship with Josie and hard-up Tony confesses to wife Dorothy that he took the £1,200 but found himself unable to steal it and hid it in a store room. Dorothy confides in Josie who helps Tony to secretly return the cash to Tate's office. The matter is closed.

EPISODE TWO
Writer: Tony Hoare
Director: Gerry Poulson
Duration: 60 minutes
Transmission date: 27 February 1988

Charisma is flattered when an attractive woman named Donna chats him up in a pub. He learns that she used to be the common-law wife of a former fireman nicknamed Liver Salts. But no sooner has she moved herself in with Charisma than he discovers from the rest of the Watch that she took Liver Salts for a ride financially. Tate is behaving irrationally and humiliates Hallam over an incident involving some missing tramps, believed trapped inside a demolished warehouse. Hallam had called out appliances from all over London but the tramps were really at a nearby off-licence. Blue Watch are called to a fire at a business premises next to a lock-up where deadly chemicals are stored. Tate warns that they must find out more about the chemicals before tackling the blaze but Charisma, wound up over a row about Donna, ignores the orders and rushes into the fire. A car petrol tank inside explodes and the fire roars out, engulfing Charisma. Badly burned, he is taken to hospital where he is visited by Donna. Although barely able to speak as a result of his injuries, he tells Donna that he knows all about her. Donna is livid that the Watch have turned Charisma against her.

Donna thought Charisma was hot stuff.

London's Burning

EPISODE THREE
Writer: Anita Bronson
Director: Gerry Mill
Duration: 60 minutes
Transmission date: 5 March 1988

Blue Watch are called out to release a lift stuck between floors in a tower block. The rescue is hindered because vandals have stolen the winding lever and the passengers are in a state of frenzy. There is constant bitching from an elderly woman about Sue, a young tart, and her client who suffers from claustrophobia. When the man is finally freed and does a runner, Vaseline wastes no time in asking Sue for a date. On their fire inspection round, the Watch visit a local garment workshop run by a Mr. Patel. The place is a death trap but Malcolm falls for one of the workers, Samina. When Tate's worst fears come true and there is a fire at Patel's, Malcolm is frantic. On the way, a troublesome pump engine breaks down and the crew's arrival at the fire is delayed. By the time they get there, several of the girls have already been killed behind the locked fire exit – among them Samina. A few weeks later Blue Watch are out in force to watch Sicknote and his wife Jean in the Penge Occasional Players' production of South Pacific. They greet his final curtain call with wild applause, especially when the fire curtain is accidentally lowered onto his head whilst he is taking a bow.

EPISODE FOUR
Writer: Anita Bronson
Director: Gerry Mill
Duration: 60 minutes
Transmission date: 12 March 1988

In the throes of divorcing husband Gerry, Josie accepts a lift home from a man she has met at evening class. He persuades Josie to ask him up to her flat for coffee but inside, mounts a savage attack on her and tries to rape her before she succeeds in fighting him off. Charisma, still recovering in hospital from his burns, reveals that he is finished with Donna and wants her out of his house. But when he is finally discharged and returns home, he finds that far from moving out, Donna has set up a ladies' hairdressing business there. Blue Watch want George, an ex-boxer, to represent them in a London Fire Brigade charity boxing match but after reluctantly agreeing, he damages his precious hands in seeing off one Big Eddie who has come to the station to batter Vaseline for non-payment of a debt. Meanwhile Tate has problems of his own. Deeply frustrated when a shout at a high-rise block of flats is jeopardised by vandalism to the fire equipment, Tate goes over the edge. He turns to drink and instead of arriving for work, takes himself off to the Kent coast for the day and gazes out to sea. On his return, he takes a week's sick leave before coming back to duty and a warm welcome.

EPISODE FIVE
Writer: Tony Hoare
Director: Gerry Poulson
Duration: 60 minutes
Transmission date: 19 March 1988

While Blue Watch are holding an open day at the station for a group of children, an armed gang rob a nearby milk depot. The gang's girl leader crashes the getaway car and hearing police sirens, the raiders rush into Blackwall where they hold the firemen and children hostage. The station is quickly surrounded by police marksmen. The firemen discover that one of the children visiting the station has stolen an EVAC portable radio and Tate manages to communicate secretly with the police outside. The atmosphere is tense as the gang demand an escape vehicle but then the firemen seize their chance and overpower two of the robbers with a fire extinguisher. Hearing the commotion, the third raider fires his shotgun indiscriminately before realising the situation is hopeless. He quietly surrenders and the firemen are reunited with anxious wives.

Christmas Special

Writer: Tony Hoare
Director: Les Blair
Duration: 90 minutes
Transmission date: 25 December 1988

It's not exactly a Merry Christmas for the members of Blue Watch. Charisma, who has been working as Santa Claus outside a West End store, comes home to find the immovable Donna selling dangerous toys. Meanwhile Hallam's odious father-in-law pours too much brandy on the Christmas pudding, thereby singeing Hallam's eyebrows, and Kevin receives an unwelcome visit from his father on the run from prison. Josie is determined that there will be no-reconciliation with husband Gerry and leaves a family gathering to join the rest of the Watch for pre-Christmas drinks. There she meets Bayleaf and the two end up in bed together. The experience is a disaster for both parties. George and Vaseline, who has slipped away from his pregnant wife Marion, have found jobs as hire-car drivers. Vaseline is so distracted by the amorous encounter of a couple in the back of the car he is driving that he crashes it through a wall and into the flat of an elderly couple watching TV. For his part, George offers a lift to a lone woman, only to discover she is a plain-clothes policewoman. Thus George is thrown in a cell late on Christmas Eve on suspicion of kerb-crawling. Luckily he is released on bail just in time for the Blue Watch Christmas dinner.

Series Two

EPISODE ONE
Writer: Anita Bronson
Director: John Reardon
Duration: 60 minutes
Transmission date: 22 October 1989

On a shout to a fire at a hotel run as council accommodation, Blue Watch are shocked by the sloppy attitude of another crew's leading officer, Dunckley. Tate criticises both the young woman whose bedroom cooking stove caused the fire and Kevin for defending her. Kevin has his own troubles, particularly with his delinquent young brother Mickey. When Kevin berates Mickey over his truancy, the boy vows revenge and starts a series of false fire alarms at his school. Later the Watch are called to another blaze at the council accommodation. The fire has already got a hold with trapped victims shouting panic-stricken from upstairs windows. Despite instructions not to jump, a man and a woman plunge to their deaths. Dunckley's crew are totally unprepared. The young mother admonished by Tate earlier is clinging desperately to a window with her baby in her arms. Kevin urges her to hang on but before he can reach her with the ladder, she loses her grip on the baby. As the baby falls to its death, she lets go and meets the same fate. The Watch return physically and emotionally drained, only to be summoned to another deliberate false alarm at Mickey's school.

EPISODE TWO
Writer: Anita Bronson
Director: Gerry Mill
Duration: 60 minutes
Transmission date: 29 October 1989

A new ADO, Scase, has been appointed to Blackwall and immediately orders a more disciplined approach. Without waiting for Tate, he reprimands Malcolm over a practical joke. Kevin's brother Mickey, high on solvents, starts a real fire at the school. Blue Watch deal with it but Kevin is deeply embarrassed when Mickey is hauled away by the police. Kevin's anxieties about his place in the Watch are forgotten when, in a swinging skip attached to a large hook, he rescues a crane driver who has fallen unconscious 200ft up in his cab. Charisma's formidable mother, back from Australia, finally ousts the unwanted resident Donna and Bayleaf falls for fireman's widow Clare. And Vaseline becomes a father.

EPISODE THREE
Writer: Anita Bronson
Director: John Reardon
Duration: 60 minutes
Transmission date: 5 November 1989

Dealing with a possible radiation leak from a train carrying spent nuclear fuel, Tate is irritated by the train's driver who demands instant decontamination. When ADO Scase arrives on the scene, he is more concerned with the driver's complaints about Tate's rudeness than the incident itself which ultimately turns out to be harmless. Meanwhile Hallam, in charge of a Watch at another station, is worried about the bullying of a young black fireman, Maddox. The firemen there, led by a racist called Scouser, wrongly believe that Maddox has complained about them to Hallam. They punish Maddox by tying him to a ladder and suspending him face-down in a tank of water. Maddox nearly drowns but does not want to pursue the matter – he has no faith in the Brigade's disciplinary system. Tony is particularly upset when a 19-year-old window cleaner dies after slipping from his ladder and impaling himself on sharp railings. And Vaseline finds that his first and third wives, both called Marion, are ganging up on him. The first wife is homeless and the third invites her to stay.

EPISODE FOUR
Writer: Anita Bronson
Director: Gerry Poulson
Duration: 60 minutes
Transmission date: 12 November 1989

Blue Watch face a race against time when two building workers are buried under collapsed scaffolding at the edge of a river. There is just half an hour before the incoming tide will drown the trapped men and Tate urgently requests a thermal imaging camera to help find them. But when ADO Scase arrives, he orders the rescue work to be halted until the remaining scaffolding is properly secured. As the tide comes in, Tate ignores Scase and the men are dragged out just in time. Josie attends a Junior Officers' Training Course, the first woman fire officer to do so from Southwark, but Sicknote is jealous that his role as leading light of his local amateur dramatic society is being usurped by newcomer Dominic. Vaseline ends up sleeping with Marion one by mistake while Charisma tries to track down his long-lost father. He is sent to the Savoy Hotel but, to his dismay, he finds that his father is only a cleaner there. He tells the Watch that the old man died a hero's death in the war but nobody believes him. Tate learns that Scase has reported him for insubordination. He has to go before the Commander.

London's Burning

EPISODE FIVE
Writer: Anita Bronson
Director: Gerry Mill
Duration: 60 minutes
Transmission date: 19 November 1989

Neither Tate nor Scase emerge unscathed from their meetings with Area Commander Bulstrode. Tate tries to make his peace and offers Scase his hand. But Scase completely ignores him. Thus Tate is delighted to learn that Scase has been posted to an obscure station in the North-East. Sicknote comes home to discover his wife Jean kissing musical rival Dominic. After attacking Dominic, he leaves home. With the Dockland Development Board buying up the area at relatively low prices, several small businesses have recently been burned down for the insurance money. Cafe owner Ray tries a similar ploy by setting fire to the building with petrol. But the violence of the flames and the exploding petrol take him by surprise and he is unable to escape. Bayleaf remembers an old man and his dog who live above the cafe. The old man is unconscious but is rescued by Josie, the lightest of the crew, after a perilous journey along smouldering joists.

EPISODE SIX
Writer: Anita Bronson
Director: John Reardon
Duration: 60 minutes
Transmission date: 26 November 1989

The Maddox case goes to a disciplinary tribunal. Hallam is called to give evidence and, despite Scouser's claim that the near-drowning was just a lark that went wrong and that the racist names were merely harmless leg-pulling, Scouser and his co-defendants are thrown out of the Fire Service. Sicknote has moved in with Charisma while George realises he has blown it with his latest girl-friend Julia. Malcolm tries to heal the rift but when George hears that Malcolm has been seen kissing Julia, he lunges at him. Meanwhile an old man has been mugged and thrown into a culvert. He is washed down into an underground tunnel where he clings to an overhanging chain for dear life. Tate orders George and Malcolm to get the old man out. They wade through rushing water and find him in the nick of time. But Malcolm trips and is about to be washed away when George comes to his rescue. Back on dry land, Tate says he hopes the cold water has knocked some sense into the pair of them.

EPISODE SEVEN
Writer: Tony Hoare
Director: Gerry Poulson
Duration: 60 minutes
Transmission date: 3 December 1989

With Guy Fawkes night approaching, Blue Watch brace themselves for the usual flood of emergency calls. A boy is left to guard a bonfire against a revenge attack from a gang of youths and in fear decides to hide inside the bonfire. He doesn't hear the youths arrive and set light to the bonfire. Blue Watch are called out since the blaze is threatening nearby flats but the youths respond by throwing bricks at them and cutting through their water hoses. The firefighters soon realise from the fumes that someone has been caught up in the flames. The boy is dead. It is by no means an isolated incident. Bayleaf goes to comfort girl-friend Clare when her son is rushed to hospital following a firework accident and the rest of the Watch are sent to a house to deal with a bonfire party which has got out of hand and engulfed the kitchen. Badly-parked cars make it impossible for the fire engine to reach the house so Tate orders the appliance to make its way forward even if it means damaging the cars. The blaze is put out but so are the guests when they see the state of their cars.

EPISODE EIGHT
Writer: Tony Hoare
Director: Gerry Mill
Duration: 60 minutes
Transmission date: 10 December 1989

Tate asks Josie to take charge of a drill. Predictably the Watch, George and Kevin in particular, are lackadaisical and Josie struggles to keep her temper. Dominic has damaged his larynx so Sicknote is persuaded to return to the fold of the Penge Occasional Players. Apart from Tony, whose wife Dorothy has left him, the whole Watch attend Sicknote's show. Malcolm thinks of a wheeze and as the cast burst into the drinking song, the Blackwall contingent join in. Sicknote is suitably outraged. The two Marions decide on a night out, leaving Vaseline to baby-sit. They return home to find him asleep with little Damian in his arms, the picture of the perfect father. Then a routine visit to Surrey Docks turns sour when a truck reverses too far and plunges into the water. Vaseline, George and Bayleaf put on their breathing apparatus and dive in. George and Bayleaf rescue the driver but there's no sign of Vaseline. He is dead. The grand Fire Brigade funeral for Vaseline reunites Sicknote and Jean and Josie reveals that Marion one is pregnant.

Series Three

EPISODE ONE
Writer: Anita Bronson
Director: Gerry Mill
Duration: 60 minutes
Transmission date: 30 September 1990

Josie is leaving Blackwall to take a job at another station. The Watch's farewell present to her is Technique, a male stripper and a member of White Watch who has been off sick for some time to concentrate on his body-building. He also moonlights as a plumber and offers to fix Marion three's plumbing. Vaseline's replacement is Colin Parrish, fresh out of training college and very green. His first shout is to a derelict shop set alight by tramps using it as a shelter. Waving the hose around, Colin knocks over one tramp and when Tate orders a team into the building to check if there are any people left, Colin enthusiastically barges through. Alas the water from his hose hits a junction box and catapults him out of the shop. As everyone clusters around, Colin asks if he put out the fire. Whilst out shopping, Josie recognises the man who tried to rape her. She follows him and his wife out into the street and accuses him of the crime. A fight ensues and the police arrive.

EPISODE TWO
Writer: Anita Bronson
Director: John Reardon
Duration: 60 minutes
Transmission date: 7 October 1990

Josie is acting as Sub at her new station and supervises a shout involving a crashed lorry carrying a load of hot tar. Two workmen are injured – one sprayed with molten tar, the other lying in agony beneath a propane cylinder. Blue Watch arrive on the scene and have to take their orders from Josie. Tate watches with pride as she organises the rescue of the two men and the immediate evacuation of the area. Blue Watch are then called out to a night fire in a ship's engine room. The hold is already full of foam when it transpires that the Chief Engineer is still down below. Malcolm leads his team down on a perilous mission because the foam means they cannot see or hear anything. Everything has to be done by touch. Eventually they resurface with the injured Chief Engineer. As a break from playing practical jokes on Colin, Blue Watch decide to do up an old car for Maggie who has passed her driving test at the sixth attempt. They park it in the station yard, to the horror of Area Commander Bulstrode who is making an official visit. Malcolm tells him it is for practising drills for road traffic accidents. Bulstrode asks to see a demonstration of a typical rescue which involves removal of the car roof. Kevin breaks the news to Maggie that her car has become a convertible.

EPISODE THREE
Writer: Anita Bronson
Director: Gerry Mill
Duration: 60 minutes
Transmission date: 14 October 1990

A drug war leads to a fire in a block of flats. Colin chases one of the suspects and is threatened with a knife. Fortunately Bayleaf has followed him and comes to his rescue but at the cost of a slashed face. The crew read the riot act to Colin, warning that his 'go it alone' approach could have resulted in a fatality. Hallam's wife Sandra is convinced that he is having an affair while Sicknote's campaign to save a city farm earns him a standing ovation at a public meeting. He rather enjoys the sensation of being considered a great orator. The Watch are called out to a horrific train crash. The implications of the job finally dawn on Colin as he and George take time to talk to a young girl trapped in a compartment. She has to have her legs amputated. Colin breaks down in tears and is comforted by Bayleaf.

EPISODE FOUR
Writer: Anita Bronson
Director: John Reardon
Duration: 60 minutes
Transmission date: 21 October 1990

After Hallam saves a distressed claimant who set fire to himself in a DHSS office, Blue Watch are called to a collapsed trench on a building site. The foreman had ignored warnings that the trench was unsafe and now a young worker has been buried alive. Malcolm uses his own body to protect the lad from a further collapse and saves his life. Tate tells the Watch he's putting Malcolm up for a bravery award. Malcolm becomes a hero and is interviewed by the national press, much to the annoyance of Sicknote whose petition to No. 10 about the city farm only receives coverage in his local newspaper. Technique is thrown out of the Brigade for moonlighting and warns Bayleaf who has been doing a painting and decorating job to make ends meet. Bayleaf has to leave the job unfinished. And George takes up ballroom dancing in the hope of meeting the girl of his dreams.

EPISODE FIVE
Writer: Anita Bronson
Director: Keith Washington
Duration: 60 minutes
Transmission date: 28 October 1990

High up on the side of an office tower block, a window cleaner's arm has become trapped in the cradle mechanism. In the absence of the high line rescue team, a terrified Sicknote is sent down on a rope. Sicknote frees the mechanism and repairs the wound but then has to lower himself all the way down to the ground by rope, whereupon he promptly collapses. Malcolm learns that Jimmy, the lad he rescued from the trench, is extensively brain damaged. At the suggestion of Clare, Bayleaf applies for a transfer, which is turned down. Sicknote temporarily takes over from Bayleaf as Mess Manager but his health food menu is greeted with universal distaste. He antagonises Maggie so much that she walks out. Technique is giving Vaseline's widow Marion the runaround. When she and some of the Watch go down to the SAS (Swan and Sugarloaf) to see him in competition, he humiliates her and announces that he is off to Stringfellows with Tuesday, the female body-building champion. A brawl breaks out during which Technique head-butts Colin but Colin's uncle Jaffa responds by hurling Technique across the pub. On reading that Technique and Tuesday have become engaged, Marion bursts into tears. She confides to Kevin that she is desperately lonely. Kevin tells her that he's always on hand.

EPISODE SIX
Writer: David Humphries
Director: Gerry Mill
Duration: 60 minutes
Transmission date: 4 November 1990

Kate Stevens joins Blue Watch and proves her prowess at an accident involving two cars and a lorry carrying chemicals. She and Bayleaf rescue a woman from one of the cars but then Kate hears a baby cry and pulls the child out just before the chemical spillage ignites. Another shout takes the crew to a man mountain named Benny who has suffered a heart attack and cannot be moved by the ambulance men. So Blue Watch have to winch him out of the window with the aid of a hydraulic platform. George's tango partner Kelly suggests he moves in with her and Tony reveals that he is contemplating leaving the brigade to set up in the boutique business with his new girl-friend Jenny.

EPISODE SEVEN
Writer: Anita Bronson
Director: John Reardon
Duration: 60 minutes
Transmission date: 11 November 1990

Blue Watch are on night duty and have been called out to a number of what Tate calls 'loony tune shouts' – a dustbin fire, a pregnant cat up a tree and so on. If nothing else, the crew are pleased that Bayleaf is back in charge of the kitchen but just as they are about to tuck in to lamb stew, the bells go down. Tate confiscates Malcolm's sandwich but the butter on it comes in handy for releasing the head of a man stuck in park railings as a stag night prank. When they return to the station, Blue Watch find supper has become a burnt offering. Colin is commandeered to fetch a Chinese takeaway but comes back with nothing more than rice and noodles. He is in the doghouse – and his snoring keeps everyone awake. Kevin meets his dad on his release from prison. The old man promises to go straight and Kevin persuades Marion to put him up. But as soon as her back is turned, Kevin's dad makes off with her gas and electricity money. Bayleaf has a narrow escape at a hospital fire when he falls through the ceiling and is only saved by his life line to Kate. And Sicknote announces that he'll be standing in the local elections.

EPISODE EIGHT
Writer: David Humphries
Director: Keith Washington
Duration: 60 minutes
Transmission date: 18 November 1990

George is suffering last-minute nerves before he and Kelly appear on a TV talent show. He only agreed in the first place because, apart from the SAS pub, no one he knows has a satellite dish. The Watch are called to a shout at an old man's flat. Tate knows the occupant but despite cutting through the old man's security door which he bought to protect himself from vandals, they find him dead in his bed. While Malcolm goes to collect his bravery award, Tate goes for his routine medical. He struggles with climbing the steps but is devastated to be told that he is to be taken off duty immediately. Sadly he tells Hallam that his career is at an end. After a call to a flooded cellar at a funeral parlour, Tate holds his farewell party in the SAS. Bayleaf puts on a video as entertainment. To George's anguish, it is a tape of he and Kelly doing the tango, specially recorded by the landlord's wife.

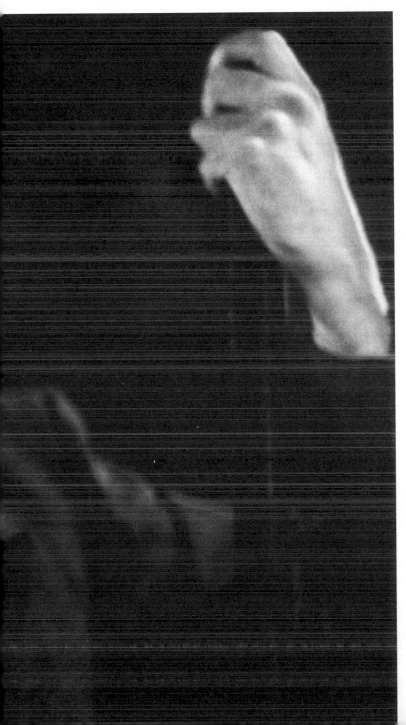

The happy couple? Kelly and George.

Series Four

EPISODE ONE
Writer: David Humphries
Director: Gerry Mill
Duration: 60 minutes
Transmission date: 29 September 1991

A light aircraft carrying two businessman crashes into a warehouse. In the process it breaks in half and sets fire to a lorry. When Blue Watch arrive, they are faced with the problem of how to make the plane safe enough to reach the two passengers, one of whom is seriously injured, as well as the dead pilot. The solution is to raise the fuselage on a giant air-bag. Acting Station Officer Hallam is being interviewed for promotion. His wife Sandra feels sufficiently confident to order a new kitchen on the strength of his increased salary. Bayleaf's girlfriend Clare and her children move in with him and Malcolm has found a lodger to help out with the mortgage – a classy law student called Helen. Sicknote decides to run as the Green candidate in the local elections. Dozy Colin misreads the address of a hotel fire and sends Hallam and the pump to the wrong place. Luckily it is a hoax call but Colin's probationary period is extended for another three months. George's girlfriend Kelly tells him she's pregnant and invites him to a party to meet her family but a stunned George finds it's their engagement that everyone is celebrating!

EPISODE TWO
Writer: David Humphries
Director: John Reardon
Duration: 60 minutes
Transmission date: 6 October 1991

A basement recording session turns to disaster when a frying pan catches fire near a sleeping roadie. In the soundproof booths nobody can hear the fire alarm until one of the technicians opens a door and is confronted by a blazing corridor. To make matters worse, the fire-door has been locked to keep out the group's fans. Four bodies are hauled out. Hallam has done a good job but it is little consolation – he has missed out on promotion. Sandra takes the news badly and in a bid to cheer Hallam up, Bayleaf volunteers the boys on the Watch to instal the new kitchen. Alas Sandra is left with a large hole in the wall when the lads forget to order the right size window frame. George remains sober and pensive during his stag night. At the reception, one of Kelly's drunken relations slags off the Fire Service and George flattens him. Then in the honeymoon suite, George gets his big surprise – Kelly may not be pregnant after all. Meanwhile Sicknote is elected to the council, to the horror of his long-suffering wife Jean.

EPISODE THREE
Writer: David Humphries
Director: Gerry Mill
Duration: 60 minutes
Transmission date: 13 October 1991

The arrival of new Station Officer Nick Georgiadis ruffles a lot of feathers. A strict disciplinarian, he finds fault with the appearance, sloppy practices and conduct of everyone from Hallam down. The atmosphere at Blackwall is decidedly hostile. Relief comes in the form of a shout to a sewer where three workmen lay injured by a gas explosion. Two had gone upstream to repair a fault but gas started to fill the sewer chamber. The noise from their work prevented them hearing either the warning from the gas detector or the shouts from their mate at the entrance. The result is that the pair are pinned under rubble while the third lies bleeding from a headwound. Under Nick's impressive command, Blue Watch free the trio. Afterwards, Nick has words with Hallam about their professional relationship and at home Sandra's nagging about the kitchen doesn't lighten Hallam's gloom. Kevin becomes involved in a brawl with his sister's hoodlum boyfriend Rick and at the next roll call, Nick sends the battered and bruised Kevin home with a flea in his ear.

EPISODE FOUR
Writer: Tony Hoare
Director: Mike Vardy
Duration: 60 minutes
Transmission date: 20 October 1991

When an elderly couple, Mabel and Sid, try to put out a fire in their old couch, young neighbour Zoe ends up calling the Fire Brigade. Mabel refuses to leave without her pet budgie and Colin, who has taken a shine to Zoe, volunteers to rescue it. As Colin endeavours to resuscitate the dead bird, he gives it a blast of air from his apparatus and sends the corpse shooting out through the open window. To Mabel and Zoe waiting outside, it looks as though the bird has flown away. Colin is Zoe's hero, to the extent that he later asks her out. The pump crew have been sent out into the Kent countryside as standby and, despite getting stuck in a muddy field, assist in fighting a barn blaze. Attempting to remove a valuable tractor from the inferno, George merely succeeds in demolishing half the barn. Councillor Sicknote has started holding surgeries in his living room. Besieged by sundry petitioners, his wife Jean grows less enthusiastic about the green cause with every cup of tea until a drunken Irishman bursts in, bleeding from a headwound and vomiting. He has mistaken Sicknote's surgery for a medical one.

EPISODE FIVE
Writer: Anita Bronson
Director: John Reardon
Duration: 60 minutes
Transmission date: 27 October 1991

Bringing a party of young children to London for the day, a coach driver is distracted by their antics and has to swerve through the central barrier to avoid a car. The coach plunges down an embankment, leaving the driver, a teacher and one boy dead and other children screaming in pain. Re-joining the Watch is Recall, so named for his photographic memory, while Colin's chosen venue for his glamour date with Zoe is a home game at Millwall. He can't understand why she doesn't answer the phone the next day. Blue Watch are called out to a gruesome accident in a block of flats where a youth is decapitated after mucking about with his mate on the roof of the lift. The blood-soaked body is discovered at the bottom of the lift shaft. Kevin reveals his feelings for Vaseline's widow Marion but is disgusted to find that she is still seeing Technique. Drunk and fuming, Kevin turns up at Nick's birthday party, held at uncle Demetri's restaurant. Kevin tries to pick up Nick's teenage sister Sophia but becomes abusive when he gets no response. Nick treats it as a family insult and floors Kevin with a right-hander.

EPISODE SIX
Writer: Anita Bronson
Director: Gerry Mill
Duration: 60 minutes
Transmission date: 3 November 1991

Two boys break into a boat moored in the marina and take out the cooking gas cylinder to sniff it. Alerted by the alarm, the security man goes to investigate. One youth escapes but the other is still sniffing and as the security man switches on the light, there is a huge explosion. When the Watch arrive, several boats are on fire. Kevin spots the security man in the freezing water and dives in without a line. Nick then has to dive in to rescue Kevin and they see the mutilated body of the second youth floating alongside them. George learns that he is going to be a father after all but Nick is fed up with the constant family pressure on him to marry cousin Ariadne. Colin and his uncle Jaffa Parrish take their revenge on Technique who has sold them a dud window-cleaning round. Marion finally realises that Technique is a rat and tries to make it up with Kevin. When he won't have anything to do with her, she takes pills and vodka and is rushed to hospital.

EPISODE SEVEN
Writer: David Humphries
Director: John Reardon
Duration: 60 minutes
Transmission date: 10 November 1991

A City yuppie, much the worse for an evening's drinking, drops his Filofax on to the track at a London Underground station. Amazingly, he climbs down to retrieve the scattered contents – in the path of an oncoming train. Blue Watch arrive to find the man trapped beneath the wheels but still alive. They manage to rescue him by jacking up the coach off the bogey. Riddled with guilt at her suicide attempt, Kevin visits Marion with a bunch of flowers. They patch it up and agree that Kevin should move in. Kate is becoming disenchanted with Jeff, the fireman she met in Kent, but passes her end-of-probation exam. A two-star hotel goes up in flames, leaving guests screaming for help from upstairs windows. Inside, Colin risks his life to save a stranded colleague. Nick is suspicious about the hotel's safety and, on confronting the manager, discovers that alterations made since the building's fire certificate was issued had turned the place into a death trap. And when a constituent, complaining about her drains, chains herself to Sicknote's railings, he decides he's had enough of being a Councillor.

EPISODE EIGHT
Writer: Tony Hoare
Director: Gerry Mill
Duration: 60 minutes
Transmission date: 17 November 1991

A builder uses a pneumatic drill in an attempt to clear a load of duff cement from the drum of his lorry before it sets. But a massive section of concrete loosens and knocks him over and another smashes onto his leg. His young son, playing nearby, calls the Brigade who realise the man must be pulled out quickly before further lumps of concrete crash down on him. Just as they finally get him out, the man dies. Touched to learn that Recall's son has cystic fibrosis, Bayleaf has organised the Watch to take part in a charity pram race to raise enough money for the boy to go to Disneyworld. It is a great success, raising over £1,000 and Maggie's daughter has managed to get free tickets for the flights to Florida. Nick has decided that the Brigade should go on a trip to Boulogne which Sicknote is organising. Sicknote throws himself into learning French but is peeved to hear that Maggie can speak the language fluently. And George has to fight off the attentions of Kelly's mum who tries to seduce him.

Recall with his happy, but troubled, family.

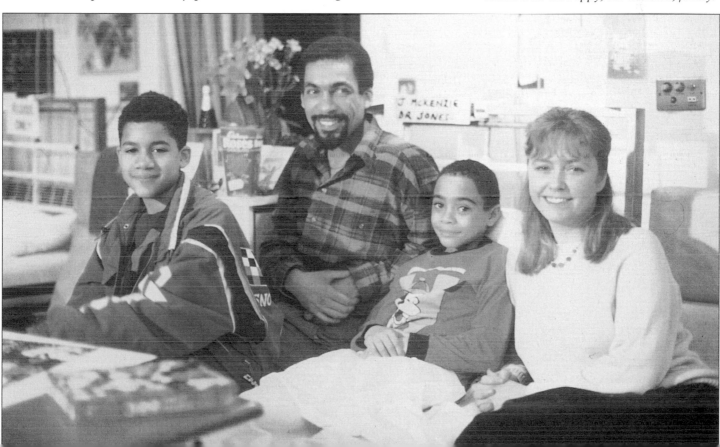

EPISODE NINE
Writer: Anita Bronson
Director: Keith Washington
Duration: 60 minutes
Transmission date: 24 November 1991

There is a surge of excitement at Blackwall as news of a massive warehouse fire comes through on the teleprinter. The scale of the incident is escalating all the time and Nick, Kate and Recall are sent into the flooded warehouse basement to find the night security man. Josie and two other members of the Charlton Blue Watch are backup. The missing man's body is found on the second floor and Nick's team are called back. But as they return, the explosion rips through to the basement where Recall is pinned down by a huge wooden beam with his air supply running low. At ground level, Bayleaf locates a hydrant under a lorry. He succeeds in attaching a standpipe to the hydrant by crawling underneath but needs Hallam's help to turn it on. Suddenly the ' building collapses, burying the men in an avalanche of rubble. Meanwhile Josie's team have reached Nick, Kate and Recall and give them much-needed breathing apparatus. And at last the vibraphone locates life in the rubble. Hallam is dragged out alive but Bayleaf is still missing.

EPISODE TEN
Writer: Anita Bronson
Director: Keith Washington
Duration: 60 minutes
Transmission date: 1 December 1991

The warehouse fire continues and a devious tabloid journalist worms her way into Sandra's new kitchen where the anxious wives and girlfriends have gathered. Clare, whose late husband was a fireman, faints when she is told that Bayleaf is missing presumed dead. However the vibraphone picks up something under the lorry cab and Kevin and Colin crawl under to jack up the lorry. They find Bayleaf unconscious but alive and drag him out to the waiting paramedics. In hospital, Bayleaf has a head injury and a broken leg but apart from that he is fine. On the other hand, Hallam is suffering real traumas. Sandra says he is cracking up and hasn't kept any appointments with the Psychiatric Counsellor. Unlike Bayleaf, he was conscious the whole time he was buried under the lorry. Hallam insists he is fit for work and has a doctor's certificate to prove it but Nick says he won't have him back until he's had a course of counselling. Nick leaves him sobbing in Sandra's arms.

5 THE REAL LONDON FIRE BRIGADE

'It was not without some trepidation that London Fire Brigade originally agreed to assist London Weekend Television with the production of *London's Burning*. Television drama can be cruel as well as it can be kind. However, all these years and series on, the decision to assist LWT can only be described as the correct one. *London's Burning* has not only proved to be a major television success but has given the Fire Service as a whole better exposure than has ever been achieved before.

There have also been positive spin-offs for London Fire Brigade as a result of the continued run of *London's Burning*. The provision of a technical adviser has meant that a series of fire safety messages have been fed into various programmes. In addition, recruitment inquiries soar when the programme is screened.

Firefighting was never going to be an easy subject for television drama, but it has to be said that Paul Knight and his colleagues have made the best efforts so far. Long may *London's Burning* continue to provide an insight into the way of the Fire Service.'

Brian Robinson
Chief Officer London Fire Brigade

Firefighting in London is probably as old as the city itself. It is known that there were firemen in ancient Rome, known as 'Vigiles', and it is highly likely that a similar force was established in Londinium during the lengthy reign of the Roman Empire. Following the fall of the Empire in the fourth century, any organised attempts at firefighting in the city were abandoned although William the Conqueror did introduce a curfew law stating that all fires and lights had to be doused at nightfall to combat the menace of thatched roofs. Even so, a huge fire in 1212 gutted a great swathe of the city and the death toll was said to be 3,000. This was known as the Great Fire of London until four centuries later.

On Sunday 2 September 1666, a fire broke out in the house and shop of Thomas Farynor, the king's baker, in Pudding Lane.

Despite the introduction of the first primitive fire appliances some 60 years earlier, which took the form of large syringes or manually operated pumps, the resulting blaze wiped out medieval London, leaving an area one and a half miles by half a mile in ashes. Although only six people were definitely killed, 13,200 houses and 87 churches were burned to the ground. Even Blue Watch would have been hard pressed to control it.

The Great Fire brought about much-needed improvements. Insurance companies were granted charters to provide fire assurances and they realised that it was in their own interests to put fires out in buildings under their cover. So they introduced new fire engines, some designed on the Continent, and firefighters were recruited from watermen who worked on the Thames. Every policy holder was issued with a fire mark fixed to the outside of the building. When a fire broke out, more than one company's 'brigade' would sometimes arrive at the scene but if the fire mark was not their own, they would leave the building – quite often to burn!

Finally the London Fire Engine Establishment was formed in 1833, boasting 13 stations and 80 full-time firefighters, commonly known as 'Jimmy Braiders' after its chief James Braidwood. But the Tooley Street fire of 1861 exposed the inadequacies of the Establishment, claiming Braidwood's life in the process, and led to the founding of the Metropolitan Fire Brigade five years later.

A Turn Out – Whitefriars – L.F.B.

10th Jul

COPYRIGHT

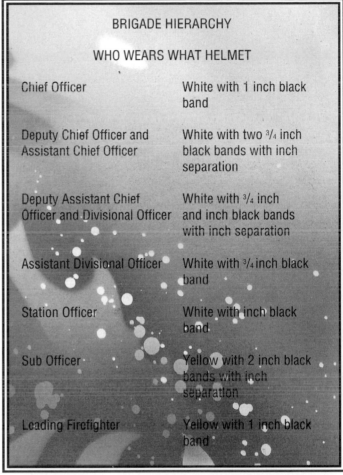

BRIGADE HIERARCHY

WHO WEARS WHAT HELMET

Chief Officer	White with 1 inch black band
Deputy Chief Officer and Assistant Chief Officer	White with two $3/4$ inch black bands with inch separation
Deputy Assistant Chief Officer and Divisional Officer	White with $3/4$ inch and inch black bands with inch separation
Assistant Divisional Officer	White with $3/4$ inch black band
Station Officer	White with inch black band
Sub Officer	Yellow with 2 inch black bands with inch separation
Leading Firefighter	Yellow with 1 inch black band

THE LANGUAGE OF THE WATCH

A.L.P.	Aerial ladder platform
B.A.	Breathing apparatus
Getaway	Fire that gets out of control
H.P.	Hydraulic platform
In the pits	In the dormitory
Junior buck	Trainee firefighter
Mickey	False alarm
Pump	Fire appliance that can pump water
R.T.A.	Road traffic accident
Shout	Emergency call
Special service	Not a fire, e.g. cat up a tree
T.I.C.	Thermal image camera
T.L.	Turntable ladder

The MFB expanded the use of steam fire engines and paid its firefighters the princely sum of 22 shillings a week. Indeed the Prince of Wales, later Edward VII, took a keen interest and at the Chandos Street fire station in Charing Cross, the Prince's fire uniform was always kept at the ready as his presence was likely at any of the capital's major fires.

The Brigade changed its title to the London Fire Brigade in 1904 with motor appliances gradually phasing out horse-drawn vehicles which were ultimately withdrawn in 1921. Further new equipment was introduced, including the cork helmet brought in to replace the old brass one which had been in use for 70 years. During the blitz, Sir Winston Churchill dubbed London's firefighters 'the heroes with grimy faces'.

The past two decades have seen a number of developments. Lighter manoeuvrable alloy ladders have been introduced, along with hydraulic platforms to aid aerial firefighting, the heat-sensitive thermal imaging camera which enables firefighters to 'see through smoke' to pinpoint casualties, and the vibraphone, a sensitive listening device, invaluable for locating buried victims. Also the traditional black helmets and leggings were changed to bright yellow to improve visibility in smoky conditions, and reinforced rubber boots replaced the traditional leather kind to combat chemical spillages.

There are currently some 6,400 operational firefighters with the LFB of whom over 50 are women. The first woman firefighter was Sue Batten who joined in 1982. In an average year, the Brigade are called out to nearly 200,000 shouts. Over the past 20 years, they have answered over 2,500,000 calls and some 3,000 civilian lives have been lost.

All emergency calls are received at the high-technology control room at Brigade Headquarters, Lambeth. In total, there are 114 fire stations in Greater London and the region is divided up into five Area Commands, the headquarters of which are Wembley (North-West), Paddington (North), Stratford (North-East), Lewisham (South-East) and Croydon (South-West). Each station is staffed 24 hours a day, every day of the year and to provide this round-the-clock cover, a four-shift system is operated. Each shift is known as a Watch and is coded as one of Red, White, Blue or Green. A particular colour Watch will rotate between day shifts (9 am – 6 pm) and night shifts (6 pm – 9 am). The same colour Watch is on duty at the same time throughout the fire service.

New recruits must be between 18 and 30 and not less than 5ft. 6in. tall and not more than 6ft. 4in, the latter restriction being to prevent them getting trapped in confined spaces. They must also have good unaided eyesight.

There is little doubt that *London's Burning* has boosted recruitment considerably. When no fewer than 11,000 eager men and women chased 100 available jobs with Strathclyde Brigade in Scotland, the Divisional Officer admitted: 'The glamour of *London's Burning* is the only explanation we can think of for the surge in the numbers of young men and women wanting to be firefighters.'

London's Burning Production Team
1991-92

Executive Producer	Nick Elliott
Producer	Paul Knight
Directors	Gerry Mill
	John Reardon
	Keith Washington
	James Hazeldine
Production Designer	Colin Monk
Directors of Photography	Geoff Harrison
	Paul Bond
Senior Writer/Story Consultant	Anita Bronson
Writers	David Humphries
	Roger Marshall
Stunt Co-ordinator	Alf Joint
Special Effects Supervisors	Tom Harris
	David Harris
Music Composers	Simon Brint
	Roddy Mathews
Production Supervisor	Christopher Hall
Fire Brigade Advisor	Brian Clark
Production Co-Ordinator	Jenny Brassett
Executive Producer's Assistant	Lin Daysh
Producer's Assistant	Patsy Lightfoot
Production Runner	Jeremy Willis
Location Managers	Kevin Holden
	Malcolm Treen
Assistant Location Manager	Casper Mill
First Assistant Directors	David Daniels
	Ken Shane
Second Assistant Director	Fran Porter
Third Assistant Director	Toby Ford
Casting Director	Corinne Rodriguez
Casting Assistant	Liz Watkins
Production Accountant	Eileen Howard-Ady
Assistant Production Accountant	Tracy Mitchell
Script Supervisors	Hilary Fagg
	Gillian Wood
	Julia Richards
Camera Operator	Ken Lowe
Focus Pullers	Mike Lippmann
	Paul Carter
Clapper/Loader	Simon Sharkey
Grip	Gary Hymns
Sound Mixers	Trevor Carless
	Reg Mills
Sound Maintenance	Charlie McFadden
Sound Assistant	Michael Reardon
Art Directors	Roger Bowles
	Rae George
Set Dresser	Samantha Selby
Art Department Runner/Storyboard Artist	Richard Kerry
Property Buyer	Will Hinton
Property Buyer's Assistant	Joanne Lambe
Costume Designer	Lynnette Cummin

Wardrobe Master	John Vieira
Wardrobe Assistants	Geraldine Gowing
	Steve Hemmings
Make-Up Supervisor	Roseann Samuel
Make-Up Artist	Jules York Moore
Supervising Editor	Frank Webb
Editor	Paul Hudson
First Assistant Editors	Nigel Parkes
	Sarah Morton
Second Assistant Editor	Paul Clegg
Dubbing Editors	Danny Longhurst
	Pat Boxshall
	Peter Joly
	Jamie McFee
Construction Manager	John Carman
Stand-By Carpenter	Steve Woolhead
Stand-By Painter	John Wall
Rigger/Driver	Ken Benson
Construction Carpenter	John Conroy
Carpenter	Kevin Hoar
Construction Painter	Gerry Knowles
Drapes	Alf Dicker
Scenic Operatives	Jamie Walker
	Mark Neeson
Publicity Officer	Vanda Rumney
Picture Editor	Shane Chapman
Stills Photographer	Mike Vaughan
Property Master	Ray Holt
Storekeeper	Joan Maddox
Chargehand	Ron Sutcliffe
Stand-By Props	Phil Burkitt
	Stewart Ellens
Chargehand Dressing Prop	Jimmy Paul
Dressing Prop	Barry Lennon
Gaffer	John Humphreys
Best Boy	Terry Maskell
Electrical Truck Driver/Electrician	Martin Duncan
Generator Driver	Steve Potts
Unit Driver	John Hollywood
Minibus Drivers	Gordon Farmer
	Bruce McCallum
Stand-By Props Van Driver	Mike Booys
Props Runaround Van Driver	Eddie Campbell
Make-Up Driver	Gary Palmer
Wardrobe Bus Drivers	Graham Fordham
	Tony Hewett
Dining Bus Driver	Tony Redman
Catering Manager	Rod Aspinall
Chef	Phillip Keene
Catering Department Assistant	Jenny Lambert